UNEXPECTED

A MATURE MALE ROMANCE

[includes alternate ending]

Greg Kauffman-Starkey

Other Books by Greg Kauffman-Starkey

A Renfaire To Remember

A Renfaire Wedding To Remember

Alpha Force: MacCullough's Mission (interactive action adventure)

Discovering Daddy (interactive erotic adventure)

Gianni's Run

Haunted Inheritance (interactive horror adventure)

Ivy (interactive horror adventure)

Kilt

Llewellyn and the Mystery of the Hanged Monk

MacDougal's Pride (interactive fantasy adventure)

My Best Friend's Father (interactive erotic adventure)

Needled: A Renaissance Faire Mystery

Not As I Do

Orion's Belt

Renfest (interactive adventure)

Song Of The Valkyrie (interactive fantasy adventure)

The Blankenship Scrolls

The Dark Side Of Fame

The Eclipse of Zycherian

The Ghost & I #1 – The Thrift Shop Mystery

The Ghost & I #2 – The Lucky Shamrock Mystery

The House on Eagle Rock (interactive horror adventure)

The Misspelled Spell

The Mystery In The Hurricane

The Silver Bass and other Stories (short stories)

The St. Sebastian Haunting (interactive horror adventure)

The Time Of After

Thunderhoof – Way Of The Centaur (interactive fantasy adventure)

What Used To Be (interactive erotic adventure)

DEDICATIONS & ACKNOWLEDGEMENTS

As always, I dedicate this work to my loving husband, Bob Starkey-Kauffman, for years of unwavering support and excellent proof-reading skills.

Special thanks to some of my dearest friends for standing with me as I weather the turbulent sea that is authorship and who help me be the best I can be.

Ken (K.G.) Follett

Martyn Wylde

Dylan Thomas Good

Ed Morgan

The Kauffman Family

and all my friends, online and IRL

One

Gerald Millard set his desk phone back in its cradle and glanced at his wrist watch. *4:47 p.m.*, it told him. It was an expensive watch, gold face and band with hands that glowed in the dark. It had been a gift from his employees when he advanced from floor supervisor to general manager at McCann's Electronics in Newford, South Dakota. He was a highly respected member of the company, well-loved by his staff. His bosses had the utmost confidence in him and saw a bright future for him in the company.

"Thirteen more minutes, and I'm off on a three-day trip to Boise for a business meeting," he said aloud to himself. He was looking forward to this, his first trip on the business's dollar, representing McCann's reputation in front of a multitude of corporate higher-ups. He was sure he would make a good showing and that McCann could be happy with him.

There was a quick rapping on his office door. The door pushed open, revealing the face of his lifelong friend and coworker at McCann's,

Merrill Bostwick. "Are you as excited as I am about this trip?" Merrill asked.

Gerald grinned. "I may be even more excited than you are."

"You did get the plane tickets, right?"

Gerald hmphed. "No, I thought it would be better if we go by car. See the sights and enjoy the scenery you can't really get a feel for at ten thousand feet."

"The weather's supposed to copperate, yeah?"

Gerald shrugged. "I haven't heard anything about adverse weather," he answered. "It's only a fifteen hour drive from here to there. That's not so bad, considering we'll be switching driving chores every couple of hours."

"You remember I'm not great on driving in snow, Gerry, especially since that unfortunate time I slid off the road and ran into a tree."

"I remember," the older man said. "I'm the one who dug you out of the snowbank and got you to the hospital with that concussion."

"I still haven't thanked you enough for that."

Gerald waved the thought away. "We're pals. It's what we do for each other. Besides, I'll be doing the driving through the more mountainous regions so you won't have to worry so much."

Merrill gave him a thumbs-up. "So I'll meet you in the parking garage at closing time, we'll dump my car at my place, pick up our suitcases, and be on our way. We can cover a couple hundred miles before it gets dark."

"Reading my mind as usual," Gerald commented. "Sometimes I think we share the same brain."

"Comes from a lifetime of knowing each other, I reckon," Merrill responded. "See you in a bit."

The door closed, leaving Gerald alone in his office. He pressed the button on the inter-office intercom. "Yes, Mr. Millard?" the voice of Mrs. Jennet Copeland, his personal assistant, came back.

"Is there anything else pressing before I leave for the meeting in Boise?" he asked.

"Just that Mr. McCann asked that you contact him before you go," Jennet replied. "I believe he wants to wish you a safe journey and good luck at the meeting."

"I'll do that right away," Gerald said. "You have a good rest of your week as well, Jennet. I know I'm leaving the office in capable hands."

"It's only for one day, Mr. Millard. I won't let it go too far off the rails in your absence."

Gerald liked her humor. She was wry but never one for sarcasm, especially well dealing with him. She was a hard worker, dedicated to the firm. The recent loss of her husband to lung cancer was devastating to her and her close friends, but the way she threw herself into her work was admirable and a good boost for McCann's. She was a good worker before; she was even more so now.

Disconnecting with Jennet, Gerald picked up the receiver and hit the speed-dial button for the big man himself's office. "McCann," the boss's husky voice said after a single ring.

"Sir, it's Gerald Millard. I heard you wanted to speak to me before I headed out for the meeting."

"Ah, yes, Millard," McCann said as if suddenly recalling something important. "Now, I want you to remember, don't ever forget, the reputation of not just our fine business but also that of my own good self is in your hands. I would go on this trip myself if not for the wife having surgery tomorrow. I know you haven't had much experience with the administrative side of our establishment, but you've shown yourself to be quite the responsible and forthright man."

"Thank you, sir."

"By taking my place, you've shouldered a lot more accountability than you're used to, but I'm confident you will do well in my stead."

"Of course, sir."

"That's all I have to say, Millard," McCann stated. "I know you would never sully the good name of McCann's."

"Never, sir."

"Good. Travel safely and do us proud."

"I will, sir. Thank you again, Mr. McCann, for this opportunity."

Without responding, McCann ended the call. Gerald set the phone down again and turned his attention to his computer. Tapping keys quickly, he opened a browser window that featured a weather map for his area of the country. North Dakota and Minnesota were shown to be destined for significantly heavy snowfall over the weekend. "Lucky we're heading in the other direction," he mused aloud. The region between Idaho and South Dakota looked to be snow-free until the following week.

Gerald closed the browser and shut down his computer, rising from his chair and walking to the coat rack next to the door. Slipping his arms into his jacket, he opened the door and left.

Jennet was gone from her desk when he passed it. He wanted to say goodbye to her before he left, but he decided their intercom exchange would have to suffice. He strode purposefully toward the elevator.

A couple minutes later, he was on the second floor of McCann's office building's attached parking garage. As he stepped out of the elevator, he heard a shout. "Gerry!" Turning his head, he saw Merrill standing next to his car, parked beside Gerald's own vehicle. Quickening his pace, Gerald reached their cars in no time.

"Just did a last-minute check of the weather so we didn't have to waste any time checking again before we go," he explained.

"Good thinking."

Gerald unlocked his car and opened the door. "See you at your place," he said. "We should get a move on as early as we can so we can get further before it gets dark."

"I'm not afraid of driving in the dark," Merrill stated.

"Neither am I," Gerald declared. "The tempertures are supposed to go way down, though. I hate steamy windows."

"Window defoggers are a modern convenience," Merrill joked.

"Funny. Anyway, let's get under way. Idaho is still a long way away."

Merrill lifted a thumb and slid into his car. Gerald followed suit, and moments later, the two men drove out of the garage out onto the rush hour streets of Newford, taking their place among the several thousands of early evening commuters trying to get home for their jobs.

Merrill's single-story house was fairly non-descript, looking like every other house on his street. Gerald had been there many times over the years, though his first trip to visit his friend had him stop at the wrong house. The young single mother who lived in the house wasn't amused at the fact that a totally strange man was on her porch unannounced.

Merrill parked his car and went to his front door. Gerald opened his vehicle's trunk and waited for Merrill to come out with his bags. The younger man returned less than a minute later with two bags, a regular suitcase and a longer one that Gerald knew housed a formal suit, their garb for the meeting.

The bags securely in the trunk, they got into the Crown Victoria's front seats and departed.

Gerald's house was far more modern and impressive than Merrill's. Two stories with a balcony over the front door and a wide porch that ran the entire front length of the house, its landscaping was immaculate and ready for the oncoming winter.

"I'll be right out," Gerald assured Merrill, climbing out. He moved to his front door and shivered as he fit the key into the lock. He walked into his den, where his suit case and suit bag were waiting for him, along with his laptop computer. Adjusting the furnace to a lower temp since he wouldn't be there for three days, he took up his bags and left, locking the door after him.

Placing his bags in the trunk alongside his friend's, Gerald got back into his car. "Are we ready?" he asked.

"Onward to adventure," Merrill laughed, pointing a finger to the road ahead of them.

Gerald chuckled as well, putting the car in gear and beginning their journey.

The city's lights faded behind them as they traveled on the interstate. Rush hour was quickly forgotten the further they got from Newford. Fewer and fewer cars sped by them. It seemed not many people paid much attention to the speed limit once they left the city as it felt like they were sitting still as cars, trucks, and RVs shot past them at ludicrous speeds.

Gerald turned on the radio, tuning it into a station that played Motown hits. He started humming along with the music while

Merrill swayed his head and patted his thighs in rhythm with the music.

By the time darkness fell and they needed the headlights, they were already outside the South Dakota state line, heading headlong into the night.

Two

"That can't be right," Gerald muttered half under his breath as his fingers tightened on the steering wheel of the old Crown Victoria. He'd been driving for only an hour after the last driver-switch with Merrill, who sat slumped against the passenger door in a deep slumber. They were well out of South Dakota but still quite far from the Idaho state line. It was just after midnight, and it had been some time since he'd seen another vehicle on the highway. The headlights began to catch the barest flittering of snow flakes. "The weather channel said there wasn't going to be snow during this trip."

He tried to dismiss this from his mind, concentrating on the interstate of him. He hoped it was just as stray flurry that wouldn't amount to anything. He looked at his passenger as Merrill shifted in his seat, groaning softly in his sleep. Gerald felt he could use the company, some conversation to help him stay awake and alert. The radio station he'd been listening to signed off for the night. He could find no decent alternative to play, so he snapped the radio off.

He cursed himself for not bringing any CDs from his collection. He was in such a hurry to get on the road, he forgot to pack any music.

Shrugging inwardly, he stared ahead of the car as miles passed beneath his tires. The snow picked up a bit as he went, but for the moment, it didn't seem that bad.

By the time arrived for the men to switch places and for Merrill to take over the wheel, the snow had gotten much harder. It was far from being a whiteout – visibility was still fairly good – but the snow cover on the pavement showed no other cars had been this way since the snow began. There were no tire tracks on the roadway, the lane markings obscured by a thin layer of flakes.

Gerald poked Merrill in the ribs to awaken him. The other man's eyes slowly opened, growing wider as he noticed the snowfall.

"Do you mind driving a little while longer?" Merrill asked nervously looking at the scene ahead of the car.

Gerald nodded. "I think I'll be fine a while longer, though I am getting tired. Maybe this is just a spotty band of snow and we'll be out of it soon."

"Thanks. I appreciate it," Merrill said, relieved. His fear of driving in snow was evident, his hands shaking with nervous tension. He hunkered down against the door again, quickly drifting off to sleep.

Gerald threw his friend a sideways smile. Merrill had been his friend since grade school. They grew up together, did everything together, and went on double dates with their girlfriends in high school. They were inseparable, being best man at each other's wedding. There was nothing one wouldn't do for the other. They truly treasured their friendship.

Focusing on the road again, Gerald decided to drive as cautiously as possible, finding the ridge where the gravel shoulder met the pavement a good indicator of the best place to drive.

* * *

The snow didn't let up until they were just inside the Idaho state line. There had been a bit more traffic around them in the meantime, leaving tire marks to follow as the morning light began to show. The mountains nearby were a sight to behold as daylight meandered over the scenery that could very well have been an artistic masterpiece on canvas.

The offramp they needed to continue their journey off the interstate came up. Gerald maneuvered down it with ease. He followed a road sign stating Boise and Ava County were to the west several hundred miles. The roadway at the intersection at the base of the offramp had been recently plowed, dirty snow piled alongside the road. The pavement was wet and black, but it looked drivable enough.

Gerald pulled off to the side and parked. He and Merrill got out of the car and got back into the car in the other man's place. Merrill strapped in and put the car in gear, moving carefully onto the road.

They traveled through a couple small towns along the route before they passed into a more rural area where the street was less well-maintained and more snow-covered. Gerald watched as Merrill's knuckles grew white as he gripped the steering wheel more tightly while his nerves began to fire inside him.

"Should we maybe trade places again?" Gerald asked, seeing the fear in his friend's eyes growing.

"It isn't your turn yet, Gerry."

"I know that, but I can tell you're getting more than a little nervous," Gerald commented.

"I can do this," Merrill muttered through clenched teeth. "I can't conquer my fear unless I face it, right? Isn't that what they say? I have to confront my fear to get over it?"

"I don't know who 'they' are, Merrill, but they can't always be right, you know. How do you know for sure that they know what they're talking about?"

"Let me try this, okay?" Merrill said tightly. "I want to see if I can do this. I can't let a miserable experience in my past keep me frightened like a whipped pup, can I?"

"I guess not," Gerald acceded reluctantly. "But the second it gets to be too much for you, tell me and we'll switch. Alright?"

Merrill nodded, eyes glued to the road ahead.

Farm pastures and fields became thickly wooded regions as mile markers whizzed by. Gerald watched Merrill, noting that the other man seemed to relax a little as time went by and he got more experience.

His thoughts drifted back in time to when the two of them were boys together, causing mischief in school and in their neighborhood, like young boys tended to do in those days. "Ding Dong Dash" was one of their favorite pastimes, ringing elderly neighbors' door bells and running to hide before the door was answered. They prided themselves that they'd never gotten caught, though both of their parents had been spoken to by the victims. If something happened around their houses, it always involved little Gerald Millard and

Merrill Bostwick, there was little doubt. They were indeed young hellions, but never caused damage with their antics but caused a furor.

More than once, the boys had ended up in a tangle of arms and legs as they tumbled down a hill in escape from someone or another.

Gerald's mind snapped back to the present when he heard Merrill give a sharp outcry. Merrill was fighting the wheel as the Crown Victoria started an uncontrollable slide across an icy patch on the roadway. Gerald grabbed the dashboard with both hands to brace himself. Merrill cried a string of uncouth epithets as the car hit a snow bank at the edge of the road, launching them into the air over a barb-wire fence into a narrow space between stands of trees. Miraculously, the car slipped between trees to come to rest in a deep pile of snow twenty yards or more into the woods.

The sudden stop of the car's flight jarred both Gerald and Merrill. Merrill's forehead cracked against the steering wheel on impact. Gerald was held in place by his seat belt. He felt agony as the belt contracted against his chest, abdomen, and pelvis severely.

A mental inspection of his body told Gerald that no bones were broken. He was sure he'd be badly bruised by the incident. He breathed a sigh of relief that he wasn't more badly injured.

Turning his attention to Merrill, Gerald found him slumped in the driver's seat, chin on chest with a stream of blood running down his forehead. He looked like he was unconscious. Reaching over gingerly, Gerald pressed his finger to Merrill's neck and felt a strong pulse. Another wave of relief washed over him as he realized his friend was alive. There was already a large bump on Merrill's forehead where it struck the steering wheel.

Gerald reached over and turned off the ignition.

Peering around the car, all Gerald could see were trees and snow. He tugged on the door's latch, pushing it open. It resisted. Snow blocked the door.

He pushed harder, throwing his shoulder against the door. Again, it didn't budge.

Mouthing a curse, Gerald tried a third time, the door crunching into the crusted snow as it moved. It didn't open very far, but he was able to squeeze his way out of the vehicle. He looked at Merrill again.

Still out.

Gerald leaned against the car, looking behind them at the opening the car had somehow flown unscathed through. He could see the roadway, but no traffic passed by.

He closed the car door and made his way through the knee-deep snow back toward the road. Twiggy bushes and brambles did their best to obstruct his progress, but Gerald fought his way through. He huddled closely inside his jacket. The material wasn't meant for extended exposure to the cold and the elements, but then again, he hadn't planned on being outside of the warmth of the Crown Victoria. He felt snow cake on his slacks, wetting his shoes, socks, and pants legs.

Up the slight incline to the road he climbed, slipping only twice before reaching the top. Gerald looked both ways, seeing no cars or trucks. All he could see was the sliding tire tracks his own had just made. He crouched to examine the road. Just as he suspected, a wide patch of black ice hidden beneath a thin coating of snow. Merrill hadn't seen the ice and was caught unawares, sending the car soaring off the road.

"Oh, nice," Gerald muttered to himself. "Just like the last time Merrill drove in the snow, except this time, he didn't ram headlong into a tree." He shrugged inwardly and sighed. "He's going to be impossible to get to drive anywhere or anything after this."

He dug his cell phone out of his pocket and woke it up. It registered getting no signal. They must have been too far out of service range. He cursed again, replacing the phone in his pocket.

He trudged back to the car, making sure to step into his own footprints in case there was something hidden from sight beneath the snow, a tree root, fallen limb or something similar to trip him.

He pulled the car door open and slipped back in. Merrill was moaning, his head moving slightly. Gerald cranked his window open and scooped a handful of snow. He packed the snow tightly into a ball before pressing the ball to Merrill's forehead.

Merrill winced and grunted.

His eyes fluttered open. He looked around him, seeing they were stationary and surrounded by snow. "I'd ask what happened, but I'm afraid of the answer."

Gerald held the snow to the bump on his friend's head. "I'm afraid it's exactly what you suspect it is, Merr," he said softly. "We've had a bit of a mishap."

"Tell me it wasn't black ice again."

"You know I can't lie to you like that," Gerald stated. "Anybody would have missed seeing that ice. I know *I* would have missed it."

"I should've traded places when you asked me." He rested his head back against the headrest, closing his eyes again.

"Then it would have been *me* with the bump on the head," Gerald joked.

"You're a better driver in snow than I am," Merrill sighed, putting his hand on his forehead, pushing Gerald's hand away from the cold snow. He held it in place himself. "There's a better chance you'd have seen the ice and maneuvered around it than I did."

"Well, that's in the past now, pal," Gerald said. "We have to figure out what we're going to do."

"Call a tow truck."

"No signal," Gerald stated. "I've already checked."

"It's getting cold in here," Merrill commented. "The heater would feel good right now."

"Sorry, I turned the car off when I went outside to see how bad our situation is."

"Can we turn it back on?" Merrill asked. "My toes are freezing. So is the rest of me."

"Let me do some more checking around before we do that," Gerald said. "There's no sense in wasting gas if we're going nowhere."

"It's not wasted if it keeps us warm."

"Just bundle up as best you can for the moment," Gerald instructed. "I'm going to do some scouting and see if someone lives out here.

Maybe I can find some shelter or someone with a phone we can use to get help."

"You're going to leave me here?" Merrill's teeth were chattering with cold.

"Not for long," Gerald replied. "I just want to have a quick look around. Who knows? We might get lucky."

"I don't feel very lucky," Merrill groused.

"Just sit tight," Gerald told him. "I promise, I won't be gone long. When I get back, we can figure out what to do."

Wordlessly, Merrill nodded unhappily.

"Back soon," Gerald said, forcing his door open again and climbing out of the car into the deep snow around the vehicle.

He took a few steps forward and looked back. His friend was hunched, arms folded around himself in his coat, watching him leave through the windshield.

Gerald made his way slowly but steadily onward, the winter wind piercing his jacket and slacks, making him quiver as he moved. In no time, the snow was above his knees and walking grew more difficult.

The trees on both sides of him helped break the wind chill pounding down on him. He felt tiny icicles growing on the tips of his mustache hairs, melting with his breath and re-growing with the cold.

The car was out of sight behind him. He knew Merrill was freezing in the car, but with the hit his head took during the crash, Merrill would be more a hindrance than a help right now. As the snow kept getting deeper, Gerald kept slogging forward.

He lost track of time. All he knew was it was getting colder and he was growing more worried about Merrill the longer they were separated. He had no clue how far he'd walked from the car, but he couldn't feel his feet anymore. He briefly considered lying down in the snow and letting nature have its way with him, but thoughts of Merrill in the Crown Victoria kept him forging on.

He forced himself onward and within minutes burst from the woods into a small clearing. The snow was falling gently, but it was what was in the center of the clearing that made Gerald's heart soar.

There was a small wooden cabin.

Saved!

Three

No one answered when Gerald knocked on the cabin's door. There were no fresh tracks in the snow, no smoke coming out of the rusted old chimney, and no sign of anyone having lived there in some time, but courtesy dictated that he knock anyway.

The door wasn't locked, pushing inward on squealing hinges. "Hello?" he called out as he stepped inside the small, dark shack. It was sparsely furnished, a ratty carpet covering the wooden floor being the closest thing to furnishing he found. No chairs, no tables – it seemed that the cabin had just been abandoned.

Quickly, Gerald looked at the ceiling and judged it to be sound. No snow was coming into the shack from above. Whether it would survive a full-on winter assault, he couldn't guess. All he knew was that it was shelter, just what he and Merrill needed.

He pulled the door closed after him as he left. He repeated his earlier tactic of walking in his own footprints all the way back to the car, where he hoped Merrill was still alright. The snow was falling more steadily now, inciting fear in Gerald that his path to the cabin might be obscured on the return trip with his friend.

This thought quickened his pace somewhat.

His heart leaped in his chest as the Crown Victoria came into view. It was barely visible with the newly-fallen snow coating it. He forced his way forth until he reached the car. He pulled on the passenger door, getting the hesitant door open and crawling inside.

"What kept you?" Merrill said, with a shivering half-chuckle.

"I found a cabin," Gerald answered. "How are you feeling?"

"Doing my best to stay awake. I know that falling asleep with a possible concussion is not a good idea."

"It sure isn't," Gerald said. He reached over and undid Merrill's seatbelt. It slid across his torso with a slap as it hit the opposite door. "Are you able to move?"

Merrill nodded, teeth chattering. "I'm not about to sit here and freeze to death. How far is this cabin?"

"It's not far," Gerald told him. "Just through those trees up ahead." He gestured toward the window, forgetting for the moment that the windshield was covered with snow. "It's not far."

Gerald backed out of the car, offering a hand as Merrill worked his way over the gear shift onto the passenger seat. He took Gerald's hand and let his friend pull him out of the car.

Shutting the door, Merrill slung an arm across Gerald's shoulders. "My leg smarts a bit."

"You may have cracked it on the bottom of the dashboard when we hit," Gerald said. "Lean on me. We'll follow my tracks and be at the cabin shortly."

He noted that his footprints was still visible, but for how long?

Gerald swatted at the falling snowflakes like a swarm of mosquitoes, trying to bat them away. Of course it was futile. The snowfall did as it pleased, and what pleased it appeared to be filling in the fading remnants of the trail of Gerald's footprints.

He pushed ahead, one arm solidly around Merrill to keep him from stumbling and falling in the deepening snow. Soon enough but not soon enough, they reached the edge of the thicker woods which helped keep the worst of the snowfall from dropping on them and hiding the path. Gerald looked up as the boughs closed in over their heads. He didn't remember ever being so happy to be beneath the cover of tree branches.

"There it is," he said softly nearly twenty minutes later. Merrill looked up. He managed a weary smile and added some energy into his step that he wasn't really feeling.

Gerald struggled to help Merrill through the cabin door. He stamped the snow from his shoes and helped his friend to the old, musty carpet and lay him down on it. Merrill gave a long, contented sigh. "No one lives here?" he asked.

"Not for quite a while," Gerald replied. "From the looks of things, nobody's been here in years."

"At least it's shelter."

"At least there's that, yeah."

Gerald spent a few moments looking around the cabin. There was a fireplace at the end of the room where they were sitting. A small iron cookstove sat beside a pantry. There was an icebox, but it was empty. No food sat in the pantry save for a badly out-of-date crackers. No water. The sink's faucet was rusted and useless.

"It's cold," Merrill whispered, rubbing his arms and legs in an attempt to warm them.

"You sit there. I'll see if I can find some dry wood and maybe get a fire started."

Merrill muttered a thanks. Gerald stepped back outside the cabin and into the nearest stand of trees, searching for twigs or branches he could use as firewood. His shoes squished on his feet with the accumulated snow that found its way in.

The snow was heavy now, nearly blinding him as he fought to find wood. After a few minutes, he managed to find a handful of twigs. It wouldn't last long, but it was a start.

Back inside the cabin, he piled the wood in the fireplace. "do you have a match?"

Merrill shook his head. "I haven't had a match on me since I quit smoking twelve years ago."

"I don't have one either," Gerald sighed. "How am I going to start a fire without a match?"

"Try rubbing the sticks together," Merrill said. "We did it way back in the Boy Scouts. If we did it then, you can do it now."

"That was forty years ago, Merr. I'm not sure I remember..."

"You were the best in camp for starting a fire, Gerry," Merrill put in.

"Okay, okay," Gerald responded, taking hold of two thick twigs. Rapidly rubbing one against the other, he soon got a spark. He blew on it and soon had a small fire going. "It's not much, but it's something."

He drew Merrill a bit closer to the fire and sat down beside him. "Not how I pictured this trip going," Merrill mused, holding out his hands to feel the fire.

"Not by a long shot."

Gerald untied his shoes and slipped them off, tossing them aside. He hooked a thumb over his soaking wet socks and slid them down and off. His toes still felt frozen, but the heat on his skin felt wonderful.

"How's your head?" he asked. He could see the bump on Merrill's forehead, the small river of blood running down the side of his face.

"It hurts, but I feel better being inside out of the snow."

"It's not a lot warmer in here, but at least it's not snowing in here."

"It'll do for now."

"Here, let me get those wet shoes off you," Gerald offered. "Wet feet is an open invitation to pneumonia, that's what my mom always said."

"What would she say if she saw us right now?" Merrill laughed.

"She'd take a switch to me for not getting your wet things off sooner."

"That's your mom to a tee, Gerry."

Gerald knelt at Merrill's side and undid the laces on his friend's shoes and took the shoes off, peeling the soaked socks off him right after. "That feels so much better."

"When the snow lets up, I'll go back to the car and get our suitcases," Gerald said. He shrugged out of his jacket and threw it to join his shoes and socks against the wall. He then helped Merrill out of his coat. "We might as well get as comfortable as we can. Hard telling how long we're going to be stuck here."

"I'm just glad we're not trying to survive this in the car," Merrill commented. "I kept imagining the forest rangers finding us frozen like popsicles in the car come the Spring."

"Not my favorite image," Gerald frowned.

He stood up and unfastened his belt, lowering his slacks and taking them off. "My pants are so wet, I don't think they'll ever dry out." He sat down beside Merrill again, clad only in his pale blue button-down business shirt and his briefs. He had to admit the warmth of the small blaze felt very good.

"I can see your weekly sessions on the handball court has treated you well," Merrill stated, his eyes scanning his friend's muscular legs.

"These legs were strong enough to get through the snow and rescue your ass, wise guy."

"I didn't mean that in a bad way."

"I know," Gerald grinned. "All the times I invited you onto the court, and you never once joined me."

"Handball's not my thing," Merrill shrugged. "I prefer to use the weights in the gym."

Gerald squeezed Merrill's bicep and gave a whistle. "Doing well at it too."

Merrill unbuckled his belt and slid out of his slacks as well. His dark grey boxers complemented his white shirt. "My pants are soaked too. I feel more comfortable without them."

Gerald's eyes traveled the length and height of their new environment. He heard the wind howling against the old glass windows. He felt fairly confident that the cabin would withstand the fury of this latest onslaught of nature's contrivance. Who knew how many years ago the cabin had been built? It was definitely constructed to last for many years.

The sky outside darkened, both from the oncoming evening and the growing snowstorm. Merrill lay back on the dirty carpet, crossing his legs at the ankles and resting his head on his hands. Gerald looked down at his friend, concerned. Merrill was looking more relaxed and much better than he had before they'd come into the shack. The firelight flickered merrily on the bristles of Merrill's short-cropped copper beard. Gerald didn't know when he'd ever seen Merrill Bostwick looking better.

He excused himself and went to the door, opening it, and scooping a handful of snow. Returning to Merrill's side, he held the cold makeshift pack to the man's forehead. The water running from the snow quickly erased the blood trail on Merrill's face. "That feels nice," the injured man mumbled, a smile crossing his face.

"Do you feel stable enough to try to get some sleep?" Gerald asked.

"I don't know," Merrill answered. "I *am* pretty sleepy, but I don't know if that's just being tired or if it's the knock on my head."

"Why don't you try to sleep some, and I'll keep an eye on you for a while?"

"Sounds good. That way, if it *is* a concussion, you can get me awake before it does any damage."

"And I can keep watch on the fire too," Gerald added.

"I wish we had blankets and pillows."

"I know, so do I, but we've got what we've got, a whole lot of nothing. A roof over our heads and walls keeping out the snow, and that's about it."

"We have each other."

"For what good that does."

"If not for you, I'd still be out in the car, freezing to death. Thanks again for that, by the way."

"I'm not about to let my best bud turn into a fuzzy ice cube, am I?"

"Another joke about my beard? I thought you said it looks good."

"It does, it really does. If nothing else, it actually makes look you look younger. On most guys, a beard makes him look older. I don't know how you do it."

"Good genes?"

Gerald playfully slapped Merrill's thigh.

"Now try to get some rest," Gerald instructed. "I'll be right here."

"Yessir," Merrill gave a mock salute and closed his eyes, hands resting lightly on his chest. His abdomen rose and fell gently with his breathing.

Gerald watched over him, trying not to blink as the night fell and the cabin got significantly colder.

His mind traveled to the business meeting he and Merrill weren't going to make it to because of this most unexpected side trip.

Why hadn't the radar been more precise? It said there would be no snow in Idaho, so what went wrong? Did Mother Nature change her mind and decide to torment the two men?

He focused on the swindling fire in the fireplace as weariness draped itself over him.

Four

Gerald quivered with cold as he roused himself. Sleep had been a long time in coming, and when it came, it wasn't deep or long enough. He felt like he'd fallen asleep in a freezer.

He looked around, recognizing that he wasn't at his own home or in the upscale hotel his PA, Jennet, had booked for him in Boise for the big meeting. He saw that the little fire he'd built had gone out sometime during the night, its meager but welcomed warmth departing and leaving Gerald and Merrill in the natural chill of the cabin in the midst of a snowstorm.

It was then that he became aware of Merrill's body cuddled up against him, essentially spooning with him trying to keep warm, one arm thrown over Gerald's torso in a tight embrace from behind. Gerald appreciated the heat from Merrill's body, but he was a bit uncomfortable with the nearness of his friend's partially-disrobed body to his own.

Gerald remembered Boy Scout camping trips where he and Merrill had shared tents when they were much younger. They stayed up long after lights-out, talking about girls and sports and whatever mischief they hoped to get into once they got back home. Gerald always felt much closer to Merrill than he did to his own siblings, his brothers Mark and Aaron and his sister Niobe. Typical brothers and sisters, they sought to exclude Gerald, the youngest of the brood, from their activities with their friends.

Then Gerald met Merrill, the only ginger boy in the entire school, and formed an immediate bond with him. They were inseparable, sleeping over at each other's houses, hanging out together at the video game arcade at the mall before an upmarket clothing store bought it out and replaced it with overpriced garments that no sane person would ever consider wearing.

The one benefit of living in the suburbs so close to the country was that there was a hidden swimming hole tucked away just inside the wooded area behind Merrill's family's home. The two boys spent many weekends there during the summers, laughing, joking, splashing, and skinny-dipping.

It was natural then, seeing each other naked. They were kids. It didn't matter. They were carefree and loved spending time together.

The last time they went to the swimming hole, it was mutually decided that they were getting too old to be skinny-dipping, just the two of them. Their interest in girls had overtaken most of their thoughts, as did dreams of the future. College, good-paying career, family. They were in the blossom of their middle teens then, and hormones being hormones, they had begun to feel a bit embarrassed being naked in front of each other. That last day at the swimming hole, they both wore bathing suits.

Gerald disentangled himself from Merrill's hold and stood up, walking barefoot across the cold wood floor. He crouched to inspect his slacks and shoes. His pants were dry, but almost felt icy where they'd been so wet the night before. His shoes were still very wet. He wouldn't be wearing them any time soon. He didn't bother checking his socks.

He wandered to the nearest window and looked out. It was still snowing heavily, piles of snow rising from the window pane, obscuring his view outside. Gerald moved to the cabin's door and pulled it open. He was met by a four-foot-tall snow drift against the door.

He shivered again.

Closing the door, he went to the cupboard and took out the box of outdated crackers he'd found when they first arrived. He opened the box and peered inside. There were maybe a dozen, possibly more, old crumbly crackers in the badly folded wax paper bag. Not much for nutrition, but they wouldn't starve. Not yet.

He heard a soft moan behind him and turned to see Merrill trying to sit up. "Easy there, Merr," Gerald warned. "You still might be suffering from that knock you took on your head."

Merrill touched the bump on his forehead and winced. "Oh, yeah. I definitely am."

Gerald walked over to his friend and squatted down beside him. "It looks like you didn't have much of a concussion. Did you sleep alright?"

"I don't know," Merrill answered. "I slept right through it, and I don't remember a thing."

"Your cheeks have more color than they did last night," Gerald commented. The soft daylight filtering in through the window was dim, but it allowed Gerald to assess Merrill's face. The knot on his forehead was an ugly shade of reddish-purple, but altogether Merrill looked a great amount better that he did when they lay down last night.

"Fire's out," Merrill observed, looking at the dark fireplace.

"I know. I'm sorry. I fell asleep not long after you did. This whole ordeal has worn me out."

"Should we see about getting more firewood?" Merrill asked.

"My pants, shoes, and socks are still wet and cold," Gerald told him. "I'm assuming yours are too. Until they get dry, I'm not going to risk putting them on and catching pneumonia hunting for twigs and such in a blizzard."

"They would dry better in front of a fire."

"Yes, they would," Gerald agreed. "We'll just have to withstand the cold a little while longer until the snow lets up."

Gerald stood and stretched, reaching both arms above his head, nearly touching the shack's ceiling, and flexing his legs and feet. He was cold, there was no doubting that, but he felt responsible for keeping Merrill's spirits up.

"We're snowed in," Gerald said. "The snowbank against the door is pretty deep."

"I could use another snow pack on my bump," Merrill stated. "Now that I'm awake, it's starting to hurt again."

Gerald strode to the door and opened it, getting a handful of snow, shutting the door again, and walking back to Merrill's side. He crouched and pressed the frigid snow to his friend's bump. "How's that? Any better?" he queried.

Merrill groaned happily. "You always have taken good care of me, Gerry. Thanks again."

Gerald tutted him. "This is what friends do, Merrill. Real friends take care of each other. I take care of you, you take care of me. It's what we do."

"You've taken care of me our entire lives, Gerry," Merrill protested. "When have I ever taken care of you?"

Gerald shrugged, removing the snow and checking the other's man's injury. The cold snow was doing wonders on Merrill's head. "Maybe before this is all over, you'll have a chance. Who knows?"

Merrill looked around, hugging his legs against his chest with both arms. "Are we ever going to get out of this place alive?"

"I sure hope so," Gerald replied. "Dying in a remote cabin in the middle of winter isn't exactly on my bucket list."

"Mine neither."

Looking at Merrill now, Gerald could still see the mostly-introverted young boy he'd met the first day of fourth grade decades ago. There were more lines in his face and a lot more hair of his face now, but it was still Merrill, his friend of so many years.

Merrill, his stand-in brother when his own blood brothers had no time for him.

Merrill, the guy who kept Gerald together the night before his wedding, making sure Gerald didn't follow his cold feet out the door and leave his bride Emma at the altar.

Merrill, who stood at his side while Emma was going through chemotherapy for her cervical cancer, not letting his friend give up to despair.

Come to think of it, Merrill had been taking care of Gerald all along, whether he knew about it or not.

"How did we get through the chill of the night?" Merrill asked, bringing Gerald out of his reverie.

"You don't remember?"

Merrill shook his head.

"We held our bodies together to keep each other warm."

"Even half-dressed?"

Gerald nodded.

"And it worked?"

"We're still alive, aren't we?"

"What passes for alive, yeah, I guess." Merrill rubbed his bare legs to get them warm.

"Kind of reminds me of when we went on camp-outs with the Scouts. Didn't we do that when it was really cold that one Fall?"

Gerald gave a chuckle. "Yeah, I suppose we did. Funny, I'd forgotten all about that. We must have done it instinctively during the night. I still wish we had some kind of a blanket or something to keep us warm."

"Isn't there a beach blanket in the trunk of your car?" Merrill asked.

Gerald snapped his fingers. "Yeah, you're right. Maybe I'll have to brave the blizzard and go back to the car. We need a change of clothes and that blanket."

"I can go with you…" Merrill began.

Gerald cut him off. "You've had a recent head injury, buddy. You're not going anywhere. I'll be fine." He was already pulling on his damp slacks and shoes. "We don't need both of us getting soaked again."

Gerald shrugged into his jacket and pulled the cabin door open, revealing to Merrill the pile of snow blocking the door. "You weren't kidding," Merrill gasped.

"I'll be back as quickly as I can."

Gerald plowed his legs through the snow, instantly regretting his decision to go back to the Crown Victoria. Snow filled his shoes at the first step, chilling him to the bone swiftly. He pulled the door shut after him and started off through the snowstorm to find his car.

Roughly twenty minutes later, he broke out of the woods and started across the final part of his trek. The car was deeply buried beneath the snow when he found it. The mound of snow on the roof was significantly higher than the surrounding snow, letting him know he was at his destination.

With one arm, Gerald swiped a good bit of the snow off the windshield and back window. He brushed off what snow he could remove from the trunk. He fished his keys from his pocket and, shivering so much he could hardly fit the key into the lock, managed to unlock the trunk.

Inside the trunk were their suitcases and suit bags. Beneath these, he found the knit beach blanket. It wasn't big, it wasn't thick, but it was more than they had the night before. Quickly searching the rest of the trunk, he found nothing else of use.

Closing and locking the trunk again, he hefted their luggage, wrapping the blanket around his shoulders as an extra barrier against the freezing winds and snow.

When he made it back to the shack, he saw that Merrill had the door open for him. He trudged inside and set their bags down, clomping off his snowy shoes and shaking flakes from his hair and jacket. Merrill closed the door.

"How was it out there?" he asked, taking the blanket from Gerald's shoulders. Gerald was already removing his newly soaked shoes.

"Horrible," Gerald remarked. "It's a mess out there. I almost didn't find the car. And the snow's getting deeper by the second. It wouldn't surprise me if we were trapped here until Spring. Not my idea of a good time."

Merrill grimaced. Clearly he wasn't a fan of the idea of spending the entire Winter stuck in this cabin.

"When you were coming back, did you see any good wood we could use to build a fire?" Merrill questioned.

"I didn't," Gerald admitted. "I was too busy focusing on getting back here and out of the storm."

Merrill kept glancing at the fireplace. "Why don't I go outside and find us from firewood?" he suggested.

"Do you know which wood will burn best, even if it's a little wet?"

"Wood is wood, isn't it?"

"Not all wood is created equal," Gerald said. He slid his numb toes back inside his shoes. "I'll go. I know what I'm looking for."

"Are you sure I can't help?"

"You just stay in here, mind the door, and try to keep getting better from that bump you've got." Gerald was back outside of the cabin before Merrill could object.

He returned several minutes later, arms loaded with mostly dry twigs and branches. He knocked on the door with his elbow and waited for Merrill to open it.

As he entered the shack, Gerald carried his load to the fireplace, set the wood on the floor, and set about starting a new fire. Once it was going, he stood up and backed away, enjoying what heat the blaze put out. He kicked off his shoes again, stripped out of his slacks, and moved over to the suitcases. "Come on, Merr, let's get changed," Gerald said. "I couldn't take another minute in these wet clothes."

Merrill joined him, peeling his shirt off.

As Merrill undressed, Gerald caught himself watching. Merrill was indeed a fit specimen of manhood. He certainly didn't appear to be in his mid-forties, as they both were. Nicely-developed abs, defined pecs with freckle-dusted shoulders, and meaty legs, Merrill Bostwick looked good.

Gerald shook his head to clear it. Why was he looking at his friend and having such strange thoughts? He'd never before thought of Merrill in that way, so why did it strike him now?

Gerald slid his own shirt off, tossing it aside and rummaging in his suitcase for a replacement. He found one identical to the one he'd been wearing – that was one thing one noticed about Gerald Millard; when he found a look he thought worked for him, he stayed with it. His closet was full of shirts exactly like this.

A new pair of slacks and socks and he felt infinitely more comfortable. Merrill was finishing changing as well. The wet clothing was left on the kitchen counter to dry.

They walked back to the fireplace and sat down side-by-side, basking in the refreshing warmth. As they sat in silence, hands out to enjoy the fire, Gerald puzzled over those bizarre feelings he'd felt only moments before. He couldn't understand them. He knew Merrill virtually all his life. Why feel this way now?

The night wasn't far off. They only had the one small blanket to cover the two of them.

Suddenly, Gerald wanted to be anywhere else but where he was.

Five

"Are you sure you're comfortable?"

Gerald was adjusting his side of the small beach blanket, trying to make sure Merrill had a sufficient amount to cover himself.

"We're on a hardwood floor on a moth-eaten rug, trying to keep warm under a postage stamp-sized blanket," Merrill replied sourly. "Of course I'm not comfortable."

Gerald blamed his friend's head injury for his mood swings. Merrill was normally a remarkably even-tempered man, usually the coolest head in the room. He had the patience of several saints. It took a lot to get him riled up. Since their plunge off the highway into the snow bank, a different side of Merrill Bostwick surfaced.

Gerald sighed and rested his head on his arm, using it as a pillow. He stared at the back of his lifelong friend's head as they lay together under the thin, insubstantial blanket. It wasn't much, but it was all they had, other than each other.

At least neither of them was trying to get through this ordeal on his own.

If Merrill had been driving by himself and had the accident when he was alone, would he have survived? He lucked out and cheated death once before during a car crash. Who was to say that he would come through a second one unscathed?

Gerald noticed the purple color of Merrill's bump had already faded to a bluish-green. Whether the lump itself had shrunk at all, he couldn't guess. He was concerned for Merrill either way. They had to survive as best they could until they found a way out of the cabin and back to some semblance of civilization.

Whoever built the cabin wanted to be far away from people. There was no doubt about that. It was far enough from the roadway and from any town that any possibility of someone coming by the shack was practically nil.

Gerald let his eyes move to the window, where he could see large snowflakes brushing against the glass on their descent to pile up on the ground around the cabin. Night was nearly complete, making it more difficult to see the flakes. He wished more than anything that he'd never agreed to go on this business trip after all.

In his mind, Gerald cursed Perry McCann's name for entrusted him to attend the meeting in his stead. Gerald had made himself indispensable to the firm and did a lot to impress the boss, so technically, he brought this on himself, but it felt far more satisfying to throw McCann under the bus for their circumstances.

"Gerry?"

Merrill's voice was quiet in the stillness of the cold cabin, almost as if he was speaking from inside a dream.

"Yeah, pal?" Gerald replied softly, leaning in closer to hear Merrill's words.

"Is it a bad thing that I'm feeling scared?"

Gerald felt a twinge of compassion. Merrill wasn't the kind of openly display or discuss his feelings. Even though they'd known each other most of their lives, there were still some things they didn't know about the other. Merrill refused to talk about some parts of his life, and Gerald accepted that. Even the best of friends didn't necessarily have to know everything there was to know about each other.

"No, it's not," Gerald responded. "You know what, I'm a little bit scared too."

"Do you think we'll get out of this alright?"

"I don't know. I wish I did. There's always hope, isn't there?" Gerald ran his hands through his own hair, trying to decide what to say. "I'm sure when we don't show up at the meeting in Boise, they'll call McCann and see if he knows where we are."

"But he won't know." Merrill gave a shiver.

"No, he won't," Gerald agreed. "If I know Perry McCann, he'll set out to find out what happened to us."

"You sound pretty sure of that."

"I have to be."

"Why is that?"

"If I let myself think we'll never get out of here, we might as well just give up right now," Gerald stated. "I don't want to die out here, and I don't want *you* to die out here. I have faith that we matter enough to McCann's that he won't let us go without a struggle."

"You have more trust in people than I do," Merrill said, looking over his shoulder at Gerald.

"Well, I'm not about to let anything happen to you if I can help it, buddy." Gerald laid a hand on Merrill's shoulder and gave a squeeze.

Merrill rested his head atop his arm. "That makes me feel a little better."

"Get some rest and feel better, Merr," Gerald said. He lay back and stared at the shadowed ceiling. "Maybe things will look better in the morning."

"It's so cold in here."

The twigs and branches Gerald had stacked in the fireplace had burned down to smoldering ashes, their warmth dissipating like a morning fog. There were precious few pieces of wood left to burn. They mutually decided to save the remaining firewood for the morning, hoping the meager blanket would keep them warm enough to last the night.

It didn't take long for Merrill's gentle breathing to be replaced by soft snoring. He had been through a lot the past couple of days. Gerald was glad his friend was able to find some reasonable slumber.

For himself, he stayed awake a while longer, looking around the barren, unfurnished cabin. It was good that they found shelter, but he was sorely disappointed that it was so grim and desolate. Still, he thought it would have been too much to ask for that anywhere they ended up after the accident would be warm and nicely-furnished.

Life didn't work that way.

He took small comfort from the sound of Merrill's sleepy breathing. At least they were alive. That counted for something, far more than where they were sheltered. When he first saw Merrill slumped on the steering wheel with blood on his face, Gerald had feared the worst, naturally. It was a rough stop for them both. He just considered himself fortunate that he wasn't hurt and was able to get Merrill to safety.

For the briefest moment, he thought about the two of them sitting in the Crown Victoria, slowly freezing to death. Finding the shack suddenly felt like the greatest thing that could happen to them.

Gerald hunkered down under the thin beach blanket and closed his eyes. He fought to ignore the chill of the air surrounding them, concentrating instead on Merrill's breathing.

Sleep soon overwhelmed him.

* * *

Gerald slowly awoke from a vivid dream of scaling the side of a snow-covered mountain. His arm was being tugged on, yanking him bodily into the waking world. He gradually opened his eyes, rapidly becoming aware that he was cuddled up close against Merrill's slumbering body. Merrill was moaning in his sleep and pulling on Gerald's arm like he was trying to cover himself with a quilt.

Merrill's body heat felt good. Gerald and he had learned long ago in the Boy Scouts that holding bodies together was a good way to ward off the cold if they were trapped out somewhere in the winter. Gerald let Merrill hold him tight against him. Conserving heat and energy was more important than anything else right now, except getting rescued.

How long had they been lying in such close contact? An hour? Two? Maybe all night?

It didn't matter. They'd kept each other warm, and that was what mattered.

Gerald closed his eyes again, resting his face against Merrill's back.

It must have been Gerald's breath on his neck that finally roused Merrill. He looked at the hand he was holding to his chest. He recognized it immediately as Gerald's.

He gazed around the room, finally remembering where they were and why. The cold morning air filled the empty cabin. He moved Gerald's hand and released it, sitting up stiffly. The wooden floor had afforded him very little sleep-worthy relief. His back ached, but the bump on his forehead seemed to feel better. He rubbed the bump, instantly regretting the decision as another bolt of pain shot through his head.

"Morning."

Merrill turned his head to see Gerald lying on the carpet beside him, half-covered by the beach blanket. So Gerald knew they'd slept in such a compromising position all night. Merrill winced.

"Did you sleep okay?" he asked.

"Eventually," Gerald replied, ratcheting himself into a sitting posture. "It took a while, what with the cold and everything."

"Did my snoring keep you awake?"

"Nah, not at all," Gerald assured him. "I actually found it kind of reassuring. Comforting even. All in all, it never got to the point of being a bad thing."

"Jenny's never liked my snoring," Merrill said. "She's always afraid there's something wrong with my lungs that make me snore."

Gerald waved away the notion. "It's fine for me," he declared.

"So, um..." Merrill began, stammering uncertainly, stumbling over his thoughts. "How we woke up just now..."

"We were taught to do that in the Scouts, don't you remember?" Gerald said with a chuckle. "Body heat conservation saves lives."

"Yeah."

"It's a big difference being doing it as Scouts and doing it as grown men," Merrill pointed out.

"Why?" Gerald asked. "Heat conservation is heat conservation, whatever your age."

Merrill looked at Gerald squarely. "It doesn't bother you? Not at all?"

"No, why would it?"

Merrill shrugged. "It just seems like of strange, two big grown men like us, cuddling like that all night."

"You'd rather try sharing body heat with someone you don't know?" Gerald tried not to sound amused.

"You know what I mean," Merrill frowned. "Can you imagine if somebody found us that way? They'd think we're…"

"We're out in the middle of the woods in a cabin in a snowstorm," Gerald said firmly. "Who's going to come in and find us? And even if we were… you know, it wouldn't be anybody else's business but ours."

"You really do have more faith in people than I do," Merrill said sharply.

"We both know we're not gay, don't we?" Gerald put out there.

Merrill shrugged.

"Don't we?" Gerald pressed.

He looked at the sullen red-bearded face of his friend and gulped. Merrill wasn't saying anything to confirm or deny his question. His friend was actively avoiding Gerald's eyes.

"Gerry," Merrill muttered, quietly, "I think I have something to tell you."

Six

Gerald Millard sat back on the floor, crossing his legs Indian-style and waiting while Merrill assembled his thoughts. He always thought he knew everything there was to know about his friend. Something in this experience – being snowbound in a forlorn, abandoned cabin far away from civilization and trying to stay alive in the frigid shack – changed Merrill somehow. What it was, Gerald dreaded to discover. He had the uneasy feeling he already knew what Merrill wanted to say.

"Merr, you don't…"

The other man held up a hand to stop Gerald from continuing. Merrill turned to look at him. The expression on his bearded face was unreadable and foreign. Gerald didn't remember ever seeing that look on him before. "Yeah, I do." Merrill gulped and scratched his chin. "We may not get out of this, and I think I need to say this, whether you're ready to hear it or not, Gerry."

Gerald closed his eyes and steeled himself.

"First off, it's not as bad as you're thinking," Merrill began.

Gerald allowed a relieved sigh to escape.

Merrill knelt in front of him and let his eyes bore into Gerald's, making the latter moderately uncomfortable. If his friend's confession was what he feared it would be, how was he prepared to react to it? The corners of his lips moved, his mustache twitching.

"Gerry, I'm bisexual and I always have been," Merrill confessed, his face turning a crimson despite the coolness of the room.

Gerald exhaled. "Always? What about Jenny, your wife?"

Merrill looked away. "She knew when we met, She had no problem with my sexuality as long as I didn't act on it. She had nothing to worry about. My heart belonged to her every day we were dating through our marriage and eventually up until our divorce."

"She didn't divorce you because...?"

"No, as I said, I never acted on it while I married to her," Merrill insisted. "It was a part of me I thought I'd successfully buried. Jen and I were so happy all fifteen years we were married. The divorce was amicable. We just grew apart during the last couple years we were together. Her career became more and more important than our relationship. So did mine, if I'm being honest. We stopped having time for each other. We ended up being little more than roommates, so we mutually decided to end it before we started hating each other."

"Wise choice."

"We thought so," Merrill continued. "Once we were out of each other's lives, I opted to move on as soon as I could."

"Yet I've never seen you dating again since," Gerald pointed out.

"Neither men nor women," Merrill nodded. "Before I met Jenny, I was something of a male whore, chasing guys and girls, sometimes spending the night with both sexes at once. Married couples who were bi-curious were where I tended to drift. I lost track of how many first-time bi encounters I was for these people."

"And I never knew," Gerald said. "I thought I knew everything about you."

"Does it make any difference if how you feel about me now that you know my deep, dark secret?" Merrill asked, earnestly. Gerald could see fear in the other man's eyes, a terror at being soundly rejected because of his revelation. They had been through too much since their childhood that something like this would tear their friendship apart.

Hadn't they?

Gerald searched Merrill's face. He looked identical to the man he'd known for years, the man he'd stood beside at his wedding and the subsequent divorce. Merrill was still the same man Gerald rescued from the snow-trapped car and bodily carried to the cabin.

Merrill seemed convinced they wouldn't live long enough to escape the cabin. The snow hadn't let up over the course of the night. It was snowing harder than ever outside. Merrill believed that by baring a hidden part of himself that Gerald was unaware of might help them bond closer during what could possibly be their final hours of life.

"Does it?" Merrill repeated the question. "Make any difference, I mean?"

"Not a bit," Gerald replied.

"You're sure? You don't seem very surprised or upset about this?"

"I'm not," Gerald assured him.

"I might be, if I were you."

"You and I have been friends all our lives," Gerald said. "Why would something like that change how our friendship runs?"

"A lot of guys distance themselves when someone they've known a long time suddenly reveals something this monumental."

"I'm not most guys."

"Thank goodness for that."

"Why tell me all this now, though? We're going to get out of this. We'll be fine."

Merrill sat on the old carpet. "We can't know that for sure, can we? We may still be here come the Spring. We'd be dead, but we'd still be here."

Gerald half-stifled a chuckle. "Be that as it may, Merr, I think we still have a chance of two to survive this ordeal. After all, the people expecting us at the business meeting have to notice we haven't arrived. They're sure to contact McCann. He'll set out a search party to look for us. I'm confident of that."

"I wish I was a certain of that as you are, but I trust you, Gerry," Merrill responded.

"So why put yourself out in the open like this?"

"Because... because I wanted you, my best friend in the world, to know... you know, just in case."

Gerald smiled and leaned forward, clapping a hand on Merrill's shoulder comfortingly.

"Besides, it doesn't get much more intimate than the two of skinny-dipping so often as kids," Merrill went on.

"Um, Merr, things can get a lot more intimate than that," Gerald stated.

"Well, yes, of course, that's true," Merrill agreed.

"You never have to hide anything from me, Merrill," Gerald told him. "We're closer than brothers."

"I know that, but even brothers have problems."

"I hate to break it to you, buddy, but your sexuality is no problem to me," Gerald commented. "You're my friend and always will be."

"Thanks so much for that, Gerry," Merrill said, visibly relaxing.

Looking around the cabin, Gerald rubbed his arms to warm them. "I should go out and get some more firewood."

"Is it still snowing?"

"Yeah, it is, but I don't think we've got much choice if we want to be warm," Gerald said, climbing to his feet.

"Do you want some company?"

"Do you feel up to it? How's your head?"

Merrill gingerly put a finger on his forehead. "I think I'm doing well. It doesn't hurt so much when I touch it."

"Okay, let's go see how much we can bring in," Gerald consented. "But the first time you feel unsteady, you're coming back inside. Got it?"

Merrill nodded, standing up to join his friend.

Gerald pulled the door open. Worse than before, the snow piled against the cabin was chin height now, nearly three feet deeper than it was last time he went outside for wood. The men exchanged glances. "Ready?" he asked.

Merrill nodded again.

They forced their way through the fluffy snow that was just beginning to pack into a more solid wall. They managed to get through a good bit of the snow and soon reached the edge of woods to the North of the shack where the snow was less deep from the trees' boughs sheltering the ground below.

Breaking off dead limbs of some trees and picking up already dropped twigs and branches protruding from the snow, both men quickly double-armfuls of firewood. They returned to the cabin, making sure to track as little snow inside as possible. Kicking off their shoes and shaking off the snow caked on their clothing, they set the wood down by the fireplace. Gerald soon had a new fire going.

As the room got warmer, Merrill slid out of his wet slacks, laying them on the floor by the fire to dry. Gerald did the same, his soaked socks and jacket joining their pants.

They sat beside each other, enjoying the warmth of the fire. The leaping, crackling flames somehow made the entire experience seem almost dreamlike, surreal in its realism. This was something neither of them had ever expected could ever happen to them.

They were glad, however, that they weren't going through this alone, that the other man was there.

Gerald found himself picturing that swimming hole so many years before and chuckled.

"What's funny?" Merrill queried.

"Just remembering the swimming hole and all the times we went there as kids."

"It was a simpler time."

"It sure was," Gerald agreed. "We were completely different people back then, you and me."

"In some ways, not so much."

"Innocence was a long time ago."

"That's true, though that wasn't exactly what I meant."

Gerald regarded the other man and blinked. "What do you mean?"

"I think a lot more happened there than you might think," Merrill declared.

"Oh? Like what?" Gerald wanted to know.

Gerald put a hand on Gerald's back. "You were the very first person other than myself that I'd ever seen naked."

"Well, you were the first for me too."

"For the longest time, I hated when we left the swimming hole," Merrill said. "It meant we had to get dressed again. It was fun hanging out naked with you, Gerry. It might have been the best part of my young life."

"Are you saying I got you started on enjoying the male body?" Gerald asked.

"If you knew how many times I stayed in the water to hide my erection…"

"Oh, my gosh," Gerald gasped.

"It's true," Merrill affirmed. "Even back then, I have to admit I was in love with you."

Gerald felt his face flush.

"I have to be honest, Gerry. I still am."

"But Jenny…"

"I loved my wife, Gerry," Merrill stated firmly. "She was such a wonderful woman and a great influence on a lot of my life."

"I'm sensing a 'but' coming."

"*But*," Merrill expressed, "she wasn't the biggest force guiding my life's direction. Why do you think we wound up in the same line of work, even the same company?"

"To be around me?"

"Exactly," Merrill confirmed.

"Well, can I be honest with you, Merr?"

"Sure."

"Those trips to the swimming hole were pretty important to me too. I wouldn't trade those days for anything in the world. It was fantastic having all those times of just you and me."

"But it wasn't your sexual awakening like it was for me," Merrill said.

Gerald looked at him squarely. "Maybe it was."

Seven

Merrill blinked, not quite sure heard Gerald's words correctly. Had the other man just said what he thought he heard him say?

"I'm sorry, I don't think I heard you right," Merrill said. "It sounded an awful lot like you said..."

"I did," Gerald confirmed.

"But you're married..."

"So you think you're the only bisexual man in the world? No one else can be ambidextrous sexually?"

Merrill shrugged. "It's just so unexpected of you."

"The same as it was coming from you."

They sat in silence for a couple minutes, the only sound heard being the crackling and popping of the burning firewood nearby. Their eyes were fixed strongly on each other's. Their lifelong connection felt as powerful as ever, but it had strangely morphed into something new.

"You've been in love with me since we were kids too?" Merrill questioned, hope surging in his chest.

"I wouldn't put it quite that way, Merr," Gerald said measuredly. "You've always been my friend, and yes, I've always loved you. But '*in love*'? I don't know."

"I'll take it," Merrill smiled.

"I'll also have to admit I wasn't quite in the male-whore class as you were," Gerald went on. "I knew I wasn't like most of the guys we knew. They were all about getting the girls. I knew I liked girls too, but I felt this odd attraction to other guys too. It took me years to give it a try. Until then, I was only with girls.

"My first time with a guy, I'll make this plain, was terrifying. I had no idea what I was doing," Gerald told his friend. "Since it always so easy to strip down with you at the swimming hole, I thought that getting naked with another man in the privacy of a hotel room in downtown Chicago would feel a lot more natural."

"The first time can be frightening," Merrill offered.

"I was on a research trip to Chicago for my college thesis," Gerald said. "I met this guy at a café. He seemed like the cool type. He was a university professor and sure looked the part. Anyway, we got talking and, before I knew it, he invited me back to his hotel.

"I won't go into the gory details, but he was nicely-built and very attractive. Up till then, I'd never seen another adult male body undressed other than mine. I... I felt spellbound. All I was aware of was that I wanted him. I needed to be with him. The more clothing he took off, the more enticed I was." He chuckled lightly. "I remember being rock-hard for a man for the first time ever.

"I must have blacked out, because the next thing I knew, I was naked and lying beside him on the bed."

"You don't need to go any further than that, Gerry," Merrill said quickly.

"After Professor Donaldson and that fateful weekend in Chicago, I started seeing my life in a different light. I caught myself observing both genders with equal interest. My eyes were certainly opened to new possibilities."

"Does Melanie know this part of your life?" Merrill asked quietly.

"It's never come up," Gerald declared. He gave a shrug. "I haven't been with a man since I met her, just like you and Jenny. It's a part of my past that I'd just about forgotten even existed."

Merrill moved to rub his hands together in front of the fire. Gerald watched him. Maybe this time stuck in the cabin wasn't such a bad thing after all; both men had found out something new about each other. It was a remarkable thing that what they discovered was the exact same thing.

Gerald Millard and Merrill Bostwick were both bisexual men. They always had been, all their lives. Even as young boys, they had known something was vastly different about themselves than the other boys their age. Their similar blossoming sex lives marked them as soul mates. Their friendship had survived a lot of things; this would be one more.

Merrill mumbled something, still facing the fire.

"I didn't quite hear that, Merr."

"I said you've still got a great body, Gerry." Merrill looked over his shoulder. "A *very* great one."

Gerald drew his bare feet up to his body.

"I was watching while you were changing clothes the first day here," Merrill confessed. "I couldn't help it. You're such a sexy man."

"No, I'm not," Gerald countered, pulling at his mustache absently like he tended to do when he was nervous.

"You sure are. You have to trust me on that, Gerry. You've aged very nicely."

"The cold in here's messed up your brain," Gerald argued.

"No, I'm thinking very clearly," Merrill said, turning to sit back beside Gerald. "You're still an exceptionally attractive guy."

Gerald stole a look at his friend. He knew Merrill wouldn't lie to him, but he was still a bit stricken by the other man's proclamation of his bisexuality and his long-time love of Gerald. "Then it's only fair that I tell you that I was admiring your body while I was taking your wet clothes off the first night here too."

"Really?" Merrill asked, surprised.

"Honestly, yes," Gerald grinned. "I was thinking how good you look since growing that beard. I mean, you looked fine before, but it really adds something to your character. It's quite... fetching."

"My oh my. 'Fetching'," Merrill laughed. "You're so old-school, Gerry. Well, thank you. I'll take it as a compliment."

"That's how it was intended, Merr. You've matured in a very handsome man."

"It looks like we both have."

Merrill leaned in closer to Gerald, parting his lips temptingly. Gerald watched him approach, unsure what to feel or do. This was his best friend on the planet. Was this the right thing to do?

What would Melanie think?

Merrill's hand appeared on Gerald's chest as if by magic, his fingers beginning to unbutton the dress shirt. "Merrill," he whispered. More buttons opened.

"Merrill, please."

The last button opened. Merrill's hand reach inside the white tee-shirt to caress Gerald's ursine skin hidden within. Gerald felt his defenses crumble.

He gave in.

"Oh, Merr..."

* * *

The beach blanket lay rumpled beneath their bodies in front of the fireplace. The fire had burned down during their lovemaking, but it was still fairly warm in the cabin despite the nakedness of its two occupants. Their bodies were entwined together, sharing passion and body heat in equal amounts.

Gerald rested atop Merrill, his hands cupping the other man's head while Merrill's hands traced erotic circles on Gerald's bare back. Gerald let one finger play on Merrill's lower lip before planting another steamy kiss on the bearded man's mouth.

"I don't know what to say," he said quietly after breaking the kiss.

"Neither do I."

Even in the chill of the shack, they had both worked up a significant sweat as they worked to pleasure each other. The smell of sex was thick in the air. They smiled at each other, kissing again.

"Some business trip," Gerald commented, rolling off Merrill's nude form to stretch out on the wooden floor next to him.

"An unexpected side trip and look what happens," Merrill laughed.

Gerald noticed the fire dying down. "Hey, I need to feed the fire or we're going to get awful cold very quickly."

"You've fed *my* fire already," Merrill grinned happily. "I guess it is the fire's turn."

Gerald got to his feet and walked the few feet to the woodpile in the corner, chose a couple thick branches and thrust them into the waning flames. As he moved, he noticed Merrill raised his torso up onto one elbow, his eyes watching his friend's naked body in the firelight.

"I love your ass," Merrill commented.

Gerald covered his bottom with both hands, turned back to Merrill, and smiled. He liked what he saw looking up at him from the rumpled blanket. Merrill was indeed a great-looking man, he admitted that much, and extremely sexy.

And, from recent experience, a wonderful lover.

Who knew that those boyhood days at the swimming hole so long ago would one day lead to Gerald and Merrill ending up in each other's arms, naked, hard, and sweaty after an energetic session of first-time sex together?

Being together felt so completely natural, something so fulfilling that he wondered why they waited so long to come out to each other. Anywhere else they might have the discussion might not have led to the same resolution – sexual abandon in a remote cabin was a great way to be together compared to having their conversation at any other location. If they'd talked in a bar, they'd have both just gotten drunk and gone home.

Gerald returned to his place beside Merrill and wrapped his arms around the other man, holding him close to his warm chest. The other man felt so good against him. Merrill's arms encircled him as well, clasping his hands behind Gerald's back.

The cold of the snow outside and the predicament that landed them in this situation temporarily left their minds as they enjoyed the warmth and nearness of the other man.

This was so unexpected, Gerald didn't know what to think about it.

Would they continue a relationship after they were rescued?

What would he have to tell his wife when he got home? And *would* he tell her?

Of course he would. Gerald Millard wasn't the kind of man to have illicit encounters and keep them a secret. But this was a *big* one!

Possibly the biggest he'd ever had in his entire life.

He was a married man, lying bare-assed naked on a cabin floor with another man. And he was absolutely enjoying it! It was years since his last sexual connection with another man, as well since his last liaison with anyone by Melanie. It was nice to know his previous experiences stayed with him to get him through a renewed interest in being with a man again.

Holding Merrill with the fire at his back felt the most wonderful Gerald could remember feeling in ages. Years maybe.

Years definitely.

Husbandly duties with his wife had been exciting for many years. He didn't like to think of it as 'routine', but Gerald had to state categorically that even though he'd only been with Merrill sexually this one time, he found it more exhilarating and invigorating than he'd felt after sex with her.

Sex with a man differed immensely from sex with a woman, not just from an anatomical viewpoint. The passion ran at a totally different level. Something about seeing Merrill between his thighs, pleasing him, gave Gerald a special thrill he'd forgotten existed.

As they lay together on the blanket, kissing and embracing, Gerald felt his feelings for his old friend deepening. Merrill had said he'd been in love with him since they were kids together.

Was that was Gerald was feeling?

Was he falling in love with Merrill, his best friend?

Merrill grasped Gerald's buttock and gave it a tender squeeze. This was followed by another kiss.

The daylight outside the window that still had a few inches not covered by snow showed that night was swiftly approaching. Even with the fire going, it was still going to be getting cold in the cabin when darkness fell.

"We'd better get some dry clothes on, Merr," he suggested. "This is no way to face a chilly night, though I must say I like the view."

Merrill spread his arms to let Gerald see him in his entirety. "You're beautiful, Gerry."

Unlike when they went skinny-dipping, both men's bodies had filled out, Gerald's developing a thick carpet of dark body hair, contrasting with Merrill's lighter dusting of ginger chest hair.

Gerald bit his lip. He was so close to telling his friend that he loved him as more than a friend. He handed Merrill his slacks, shirt, and underwear before pulling his own clothing on.

Soon, night was complete, and the cabin was dark except for the flickering flame in the fireplace. The men sat together in its light, the beach blanket draped across their shoulders. Merrill had an arm around Gerald's waist.

Both wondered what the next day would bring. What did life still have in store for them?

Eight

Gerald roused himself the next morning, finding himself still in Merrill's arms. The events of the previous evening came flooding back. He winced. How could he have done what he did, making love with his oldest and best friend? Up until yesterday, they had never been a solitary hint that there was any form of erotic attraction between them. Yet, here they lay, two men – both of them considering the other to be one hundred percent straight all their lives – embracing through the wintery night after an exciting, somewhat awkward but extraordinarily eye-opening sexual awakening.

His mind went immediately to Melanie, his wife of twenty-some years. Gerald never had an affair since he got together with the incredible beauty. No other woman ever caught his eye the way she did.

Merrill was no woman, that was painfully obvious from the experience in front of the fireplace. Should he feel the shame he would normally feel if dallying with a woman since his recent, unexpected encounter with Merrill? Somehow, it felt like a completely different moral problem. Gerald had sworn off sex with other women when he took Melanie to be his bride. But, again, Merrill wasn't a woman.

Being with Merrill in a way that was far deeper than friendship made Gerald feel strange inside. Sure, the two had been naked together in their youth during their skinny-dipping excursions to the swimming hole, and he was moderately used to undressing in front of other guys in the changing room and showers at the local health club, but last night was a different animal altogether.

Gerald hadn't gotten an erection for a man since his more libidinous time during his college days when he was in his sexual experimentation stage. It was a time he felt was best left in the past, no longer relevant to who he was once he was a happily married man.

He looked into Merrill's sleeping face, so peaceful in slumber, so near to his own. Their noses nearly touched. Merrill Bostwick was a handsome man as the morning light filtered in through the window nearby. The bristles of his copper-red beard shone in the growing light.

Gerald wanted so much to kiss him, awaken him like a fairy tale princess. He yearned to press his lips to Merrill's, to spark again what they felt last night. The fire inside him replaced the fire in the fireplace that had long since dwindled out, leaving the cabin as cold as it was when they first stumbled through the door.

Merrill felt good in his arms. That was a fact Gerald couldn't deny. For the slightest moment, he let himself think that Merrill felt better against him than Melanie ever had.

He quickly shrugged off that notion.

He carefully maneuvered out of Merrill's arms and stood up, walking to the cupboard. Taking the ancient box of crackers from the shelf, he guessed there were maybe four left in the package. They had each only had one cracker per day since they were in the cabin, and the rumbles in Gerald's stomach were growing more intrusive into his thoughts. They needed to get out of there soon. He set the box on the counter and crossed the room to the window. Peering out, Gerald noticed that the snow had stopped falling during the night. However, the snow against the wall of the house nearly reached the top of the window.

"Gerry?"

The sleepy voice caused Gerald to turn back into the cabin. Merrill had rolled onto his back and was looking up at him. A contented smile was pasted across his face.

"How do you feel? Did you sleep alright?" Gerald asked, returning to his friend's side.

"I'm feeling much better. My head doesn't hurt anymore," Merrill told him. "I think I slept the best I've slept in a long, long time."

"Snow's stopped," Gerald reported.

"Good. Should we get another fire started?"

"That's my next project," Gerald said. "If nothing else, it will make a smoke plume to let people know we're here. It may be our only hope of being rescued."

Merrill nodded.

He watched as Gerald added twigs to the pile of burnt wood in the fireplace and worked to get it aflame, noting particularly the way Gerald's pants stretched across his bottom when he crouched down.

In no time, the cabin was getting somewhat warm again. Merrill put out his hands to welcome the warmth.

Gerald took his place beside the other man again. He didn't say a word, his attention divided between the new fire and listening to Merrill's breathing next to him.

Replaying their activities the night before through his mind, Gerald wondered what was going to happen between them now. Would they remain the close friends they'd always been? Would having had sex together make a damaging change in their friendship? What would happen to his marriage to Melanie?

"You're awfully quiet."

Gerald turned his head to look at Merrill. He would be hard-pressed to think of a time when his friend had looked so vital and healthy, especially since the divorce when Merrill chose to let himself go a bit.

Concentrating on Merrill's face, he noticed that the lump on his forehead was smaller than it was yesterday. He allowed himself a small smile of relief that Merrill was feeling better.

"I'm just thinking," Gerald answered presently.

"About last night?"

Gerald nodded.

"So am I," Merrill stated. "I can't get it out of my brain."

"Me neither."

"But not in the same way I am, am I right?"

Gerald gave a shrug. "I have no idea how to answer that, Merr. To be honest, I'm not sure exactly who I am anymore. I'm not sure that was me last night."

"You're Gerald Millard, one of the greatest men I've ever had the privilege to know."

"I'm a married man, Merr," Gerald countered. "What we did last night ripped apart everything my marriage stands for. I promised to forsake all others. In my mind, that should have included my best friend."

"I know you're married, Gerry. I was there as your best man. What did we do that's so wrong?"

"I had sex with someone who isn't my wife, for one thing," Gerald exclaimed. "How can I ever forgive myself for such an indiscretion against her?"

Merrill focusing his gaze on the fire.

"You regret last night, don't you?" he asked.

"Damn right, I do," Gerald said. "It should never have happened, regardless of the mutual attraction we felt. And I definitely felt it, but I love Melanie."

"And I love you!" Merrill's face swiftly turned to look at Gerald, his four words cutting deep into his friend with an alarming ferocity that startled them both.

Gerald looked away.

"I love you too," he whispered.

"I didn't quite hear that."

"I said I love you too, damn me to hell. I love you too, Merrill. There I've said it. Damn me..." Hot tears started rolling down Gerald face. He covered his face with both hands and lay back on the floor, deep sobs shaking his body.

"Damn me, I love you..."

"How is that a bad thing, Gerry? Tell me that. How is loving your best friend a bad thing?" Merrill shifted to lie down beside Gerald.

Gerald said nothing, just heaved with more sobs.

Merrill reached out and stroked Gerald's dark hair. He decided to let whatever was bothering his friend run its course. Sometime soon, Gerald would be able to talk again.

"I'm a monster," Gerald cried.

"You're no monster, Gerry. You're a man. There's nothing wrong with being a man. Men have needs."

Gerald moved his hands to look at Merrill. "Only a monster would do what I've done to Melanie."

"You've done nothing to Melanie, Gerry," Merrill said. "What you did, you did to me, and very well if I may say so."

Gerald covered his face again, rolling his body away from Merrill. "I've broken a sacred marriage vow. Don't even try to tell me otherwise."

"No, I won't do that," Merrill said. "I don't even feel equipped to make an argument like that."

"I'm sorry, so sorry. None of this should have ever happened. Never, never…"

"It was under some pretty extreme circumstances, Gerry," Merrill told him. "Under normal conditions, I honestly don't think we'd have even confided our secret bisexuality to each other. Under normal conditions, we sure wouldn't have undressed for each other."

"No, the hell not." Gerald was sounding more harshly frustrated by events the more they talked. "Even best friends should have things they don't know about each other, do what we've done. You don't understand. You were never supposed to know about my bisexuality, Merr. The past is supposed to stay in the past where it belongs. Things I did when I was younger aren't even supposed to exist anymore. Having sex with men is supposed to be something I don't *do* anymore. Period.

"Yet here we are. We did what we did. We can't deny it and can't take it back. It happened. It shouldn't have, but it did."

"I, for one, am kind of glad it did."

Gerald turned over and stared at Merrill. "You're glad I betrayed my wife?"

"Not that, no," Merrill answered.

"Then what?" Gerald sat up, eyes full of desperate pleading.

"I'm glad, for one thing, that there will never be any sexual tension between us again."

"There wasn't any before, not that I was aware of. I didn't know about you. You didn't know about me. It was perfect."

"You haven't been in love with you since we were kids," Merrill pointed out. "I've wanted you for so many years, I've lost count. Getting you into a sexual situation was something I'd always wanted, longed for. Lusted for."

"Well, good for you, Merr, you've had a dream come true.. Oh, happy day!"

"If you think about it, Gerry, it was a test of our friendship, and I'd like to think we both passed." Merrill was smiling, forcing Gerald to look away again.

"It seems to me that succumbing to lustations for each other would be considered a failure, not a success, Merr. It's not how life is supposed to work."

"You're looking at it from the wrong angle."

"I'm looking at it from the only angle I can see, that of a man who cheated on his wife with another man, my own best friend. What other angle *is* there?"

"You're going to tell me you didn't want me too last night?" Merrill's voice dripped with skepticism.

Gerald clamped his lips shut. He knew what answer Merrill was fishing for. He didn't want to give it.

"Tell me I'm wrong, Gerry. Just those two words 'you're wrong', is all you have to say."

"I can't."

Gerald turned his back to Merrill, stood up and crossed to the cabin's door. The air at that end of the room was far cooler than it was on the old musty carpet. He opened the door, faced by the tall mound of snow waiting there. He scooped a handful and rubbed it on his face. The chill of the fresh snow distracted his mind for a few short moments.

He looked out over the top of the snow. Gerald let his mind soar back to Newford, South Dakota, to the small house he shared with Melanie. He remembered their wedding night, the first time they truly gave themselves to each other. Promises were made that night.

Promises were also made between two young boys as they frolicked in the swimming hole many years ago. They vowed to always be there for the other, no matter what the circumstances, no matter where or when.

Was there something special about a promise made while naked?

Did it make any difference? He didn't see how.

Gerald recalled the first thoughts in his head upon waking up that morning. He was in Merrill's arms, thinking how beautiful the other man was and how much he wanted to kiss him.

His face flushed again. He rubbed another handful of snow onto his skin, hoping to stop the flare of feelings overwhelming him.

Merrill stood up and joined him at the door. Gentle breeze came in, several large flakes accompanying it. The men stood still, both lost in their own thoughts.

Merrill lifted a hand and rested it on Gerald's shoulder. Gerald flinched. The contact disturbed him, but it also felt good to him. Comfortable, yet uncomfortable. He couldn't tell. Merrill had stood by him through so much of his life. He couldn't imagine ever trying to live in a world where Merrill didn't exist. Gerald put a hand over Merrill's hand and clutched it tightly. He turned and looked deep into his friend's eyes.

"I'm sorry."

"There's nothing to be sorry about, Gerry," Merrill said softly. "It's probably natural to have this kind of reaction after what we did. It was strange circumstances."

"I still feel like I've irreparably ruined my marriage by being with you... that way." Tears were fighting to run down his face again.

"Men do unusual things in the name of friendship sometimes, Gerry."

"That doesn't make us having sex the right thing to do, does it?"

"No, it does not," Merrill said, shaking his head.

"But you'd do it again."

"Yes, I would."

Gerald gripped his friend's hands, enjoying their warmth. He searched Merrill's face in silence for a few minutes. He saw nothing earnest love on the other man's face. This man meant the world to him and had for a good many years. There was nothing they wouldn't do for each other.

Nothing.

Gerald gulped deeply.

"So would I."

He reached out and pulled Merrill into a long, deep, hard hug. Merrill happily returned it, clasping Gerald's beefy body to his own.

They both began to weep.

Nine

"What's it look like out there?"

Merrill came up behind Gerald who was standing at the open doorway, staring out at the mounds of whiteness punctuated at irregular intervals with trees and snow-covered bushes. If it had been under other circumstances, he would have thought the scenery was beautiful, like something off a Currier and Ives postcard. The unearthly monochromatic world outside the cabin made him feel as if he was trapped within a waking dream.

Out of sight beyond the hedge of trees before him sat the Crown Victoria, entrenched in a snowbank, having unceremoniously skidded off the highway to a shuddering, sudden stop. Gerald had no notion whether the car could still be seen from the road, but he hoped it wasn't as snowed under as the cabin was.

Merrill's head wound seemed to be healing nicely. There was barely a lump on his forehead anymore, and just a little discoloration of his flesh. The hit he took on the steering wheel had worried them both, but it proved less a danger than they'd originally feared. To be sure he was healing alright, they kept occasional snow packs on the bump. So far, it appeared to have helped shrink the lump.

Both men felt better about that.

Gerald was keenly aware of his friend's hand on his shoulder. He appreciated the warmth and the feeling, though he continued to feel an odd sense of dread in the pit of his belly. He knew that, after this weekend, his life wasn't going to be the same.

He and his best friend had had sex.

It seems a lot to wrap his head around. Of course, he enjoyed the sensual intensity while they were together, naked and uninhibited for the first time in lifetime of their friendship. The times they were nude together as young boys was an entirely different thing, in spite of the fact that it was still the same two of them, Gerald and Merrill, the same bodies just decades older and much more aware of sexuality. Skinny-dipping in a pond was vastly different than pleasuring each other on an old rug in front of a crackling fire.

There was no innocence now.

It was all done with a purpose. They couldn't even use the excuse of holding each other close to share body heat. They succumbed to an erotic electricity that neither wanted to control.

Once it started, there was no stopping it.

"The world is still out there."

"It looks like the snowstorm is over with," Merrill commented.

"There must be six feet of snow on the ground," Gerald replied. "How will we know where the tripping hazards are? We could end up with twisted ankles, broken legs, or what have you if we try to make it to the road to flag down help." He took a vicious swipe at the snowbank blocking the door, sending a small avalanche tumbling onto the cabin's floor.

"They have to be missing by now."

"Fat lot of good it does," Gerald groused. "We missed the meeting. Old man McCann's probably already popping his arteries, stressing out over us."

"With luck, the administrators from the meeting have already told him we didn't show. For all we know, McCann may have started a search for us."

Gerald gave a dismissive shrug.

Merrill regarded him with a cocked eyebrow. Gerald was acting unnaturally irritated. His body was tensed like a coiled spring, ready to bounce. Merrill felt Gerald's shoulder muscles seize up in his hand. "Okay, what's wrong, Gerry? I can tell something's bothering you more than the depth of the snow outside."

Gerald said nothing, continuing to stare out the door. The woods seemed impenetrable, determined to keep the men from escaping the clutches of the lonely, deserted shack. He'd been back to the car twice already: once to bring Merrill into the shelter of the building; and once to get their luggage so they didn't have to sit in the cold wearing wet clothing.

Now it appeared a third trip would be impossible. The tree line seemed to close itself off into a solid wall as if by some arcane magic.

"Gerry? Talk to me. What's going on with you?"

Gerald turned. His eyes met Merrill's.

"It's nothing."

"That's bull," Merrill retorted. "I haven't seen you this tense since you were in line for that promotion a few years ago. It turned out you were worrying for no reason. You were a dead cert for the position, and you got it."

"This isn't then."

"No kidding."

Gerald lifted a hand and caressed Merrill's whiskery cheek. "This is now. An entirely new now than I ever dreamed I'd be living in."

Merrill laid his hand on Gerald's. "You're still having trouble with the two of us having sex."

Gerald retracted his hand. "Why wouldn't I be? I mean, I haven't been that guy in years, decades even."

"When we get home, you don't have to be 'that guy' anymore, Gerry," Merrill said. "I'm not going to deny it happened nor will I say that it wasn't one of the greatest things that ever happened to me, but you don't need to shoulder all the blame for it. I came onto you, remember? I made the first move."

"And I gave in. I let it happen."

"I know."

"It wouldn't have happened at all if... if I didn't want it to," Gerald said unsteadily. "That's the biggest problem with what happened, Merr." He looked his friend in the eyes again. "I think I wanted it as much as you did, heaven help me. For all my fears and whys and wherefores, I wanted you."

"You were so adorably frightened."

"I *wasn't* frightened," Gerald countered. "I was just, um... just out of practice. Like I said, I hadn't been with a man since I met Melanie. It's been so many years, Merr."

"It's like a bicycle, Gerry. Once you learn..."

Gerald laughed. "I can't believe you pulled out that ancient bicycle saying. You're starting to show your age, buddy."

"Well, I'm just saying that you took to it like a duck to water," Merrill stated.

"You're full of clichés today."

"Alright, Gerry, how would *you* say you got back into sex with another man? Hmm?"

Gerald thought for a long moment. He shrugged. "I have no words for it."

"It felt natural, right? It felt exactly the same as you remembered it did, didn't it?"

"No guy I was ever with felt like you."

"And why is that?"

"None of them were my best friend."

"And that made a difference how?"

"Because it was a part of our friendship we'd never visited before," Gerald declared. "Sex between us was never a 'thing' before. We were always friends, there for each other, Hell or high water."

"And we still can be."

"But it's different now."

"How is it different? We're the same guys we were before we made this trip. You're still you, and I'm still me. Gerald and Merrill, best friends forever."

"But it's all changed now."

"Because we've had sex?"

Gerald nodded.

"In my book, I think that makes us even better friends," Merrill stated. "To me, that cements us even closer."

"I guess I'm still reeling from how unexpected all this has been," Gerald confided. "It's a lot to take in. I mean, I never suspected you were bi and into men as well as women."

"So are you."

"Yeah, but that's me. I know me. The only one who knows me anywhere near as well as I know myself is you, Merr. You and Melanie. I know what I'm capable of sexually. Lord knows I had enough practice before I met my wife. But I never had any reason to think about you that way."

"I've been thinking of you sexually for quite a few years, Gerry."

"So you tell me."

"If I can make a comment about being with you sexually…"

"Oh, I'd really rather you didn't."

"… You've exceeded all my fantasies' expectations, Gerry," Merrill told him. "I always hoped you'd be good in bed. Having finally got you, I can say you're better than good. By leaps and bounds better." Gerald blushed despite the cool breeze coming in the door.

"Now I know you're full of crap." He had an amused but still skeptical look on his face.

"No, I'm being totally honest, Gerry." Merrill took Gerald's hands in his own. "I would never lie to my best friend in the world. If you love and respect someone, you don't lie to them."

Gerald bowed his head, feeling unworthy of his companion's words. "Can I be honest with you too, Merr?"

"Of course."

"You were pretty fantastic yourself." He pulled his friend into another strong hug. Their affection felt so wonderful to them both.

"I have to admit, as sudden as it happened and all, I liked how you felt against me too. I didn't anticipate enjoying being with a man in such a physical way again. But I need to say that I'm glad it was with you, Merr. If I was going to get back into making love with a guy, my best friend couldn't be a better choice."

"My thought precisely." They broke the embrace and stood looking at each other.

"I do love you, Merrill."

"And I love you, Gerry, very very much."

They squeezed each other's hands, smiling.

"Telling Melanie about this isn't going to be easy," Gerald said sadly.

"Why tell her at all?" Merrill asked. "It has nothing to do with her."

"Every part of my life has something to do with her, Merr," Gerald argued. "She's my wife. You said yourself that if you love and respect someone, you don't lie to them. Melanie earned my love and trust and respect years ago. I can't lie to her."

"I guess you're right," Merrill said. "I would have told Jenny too, if I was still married to her. As far as she's concerned, our accidentally sordid weekend isn't any of her business."

"I don't have that luxury. I'm still married to my wife and I love her so much."

"I'm not saying you don't or you shouldn't," Merrill told him. "I know Melanie, and I know she's a wonderful woman. You're lucky to have her, and she's lucky to have you."

"Why am I not feeling so lucky right now?"

"You haven't justified what we did in your conscious yet. It may happen. It may not. That's up to you and how you want to face the situation. For me, I'm going to treasure it forever in my memory. Something I'd longed for for years actually finally happened, and I have no intention of forgetting it."

"To tell the truth, I won't forget it either. Even with all the experiences I had in the past with men, women, even couples, none have honestly made me feel the way you've made me feel."

"Is that a good or a bad thing?" Merrill asked.

Gerald put his arms around Merrill's neck. "A very good thing."

"You're having trouble keeping your emotions in line, Gerry."

"I'm still confused by a lot of what's happened, but I will do my best with it as I'm able. You've meant the world to me all my life, been my best friend, my cohort, my confidante when I needed one. I would almost say you're the best part of me, Merr. I'm fortunate you've stayed by me for so long."

"It's been my pleasure."

They both laughed.

"What say we try to figure out a way out of this mess?" Gerald suggested.

"I'm open to ideas."

"First, help me scoop some of this snow aside so we can at least get out of the cabin. Then we'll consider our next move."

Ten

Gerald stomped the snow off his shoes, flexing his toes inside them to try to get warmth back into them. He had spent the last half hour outside the cabin, walking through the snow and writing the word "HELP". Despite the snowstorm having passed, the temperature was still colder than he liked to be outdoors in.

While Gerald was making the distress sign, Merrill shoveled a short path through the snowbank in front of the cabin, using his arms as shovels as best he could. He made decent progress, going about twenty feet out into the bank and digging as deeply as he could, wide enough for the men to walk through. By the time he'd finished, his fingers were so cold, he could barely bend them.

Gerald started a fire with the last of their collected wood, and sat Merrill down in front of it, taking his place beside him. Merrill put his hands close to the flames for warmth. Gerald doffed his shoes and socks, putting his chilled feet near the fire as well.

Several times, they exchanged glances, sharing a smile or two. Gerald decided that Merrill was right. In spite of everything, he truly felt the two of them had become closer during this journey. He deeply loved his friend – he always had, but he hadn't known just how deep his feelings for Merrill ran until it was put to the test in the frigid cabin.

"Do you think the sign will work?" Merrill asked.

"I have no way of knowing really," Gerald replied. "They do it in all those shipwreck movies. I don't know if we're on any flight paths. I just have to keep positive and hope someone flies overhead and sees it."

"I got as far as I could making a path before I couldn't go any further."

"You did your best," Gerald said, clapping Merrill on the back.

"You know we're down to the last stale crackers in that carton," Merrill pointed out. "One cracker each for the past two days hasn't been very filling."

"We work with what we've got. I'm seriously lusting for a big steak and potato dinner."

"Oh, you had to say something like that," Merrill moaned, rubbing his complaining stomach. "Now I'm hungrier than ever."

"Sorry," Gerald chuckled.

Gerald reached over and kneaded his friend's cold hands. "I can almost feel that," Merrill joked. "I might be getting some feeling back."

They sat and watched the fire dance in the fireplace. The whole experience had opened their eyes, and they were sure life was going to take some getting used to after this.

* * *

Neither of them remembered falling asleep, but they awoke leaning against each other with the beach blanket draped over their shoulders. A loud clamor sounded behind them. They spun around to see three men in heavy coats and snow boots push the door open and enter the cabin.

"We've got people in here," one of them shouted out the door. It was then that Gerald recognized that the men were police officers.

Two of the men charged across the floor and knelt down beside them. "Any injuries? Are you hurt?" one of them asked.

"I had a knock to the head when the car went off the road, but I'm doing better," Merrill answered. The officer checked Merrill's eyes and examined what was left of his bump.

"What about you, sir?" the other officer asked Gerald.

"Do cold toes count as an injury?"

"You know, you two are very lucky," the first officer said. "Someone reported seeing a car in the ditch a couple days ago. We couldn't get a search party out here in that storm. Visibility might as well have been total white-out. Everything stopped everywhere."

"Is that typical in Idaho?" Gerald asked.

"Pretty much, most years, though this winter might have set a new record for sub-zero temperatures."

"I'm not surprised," Merrill put in.

"Are you gentlemen Gerald Millard and Merrill Bostwick?"

"That's us."

"Your boss, Perry McCann, has been a very worried mess, wondering what happened to you guys," the second officer said.

"He set out the search party for us?" Gerald asked.

"He and the state police combined got us mobilized," the first officer stated. "You're long overdue for some business meeting in Boise apparently."

"I don't drive well in snow," Merrill admitted. "I was at the wheel when we went off the highway."

"You drove well enough if the two of you are still alive."

"We're alive because Gerry here was able to get out of the car and find this cabin," Merrill said, giving Gerald a fond look. "I'd probably have frozen to death in the car if he hadn't."

"Resourcefulness runs in my family," Gerald cracked. "Luckily I wasn't hurt in the accident and could carry him all this way."

"That's remarkable."

The cops exchanged glances. The man by the door ushered in a paramedic, who set to work checking both men over for hidden injuries.

"I'm surprised this head injury is doing so well," the lady paramedic said. "He must have gotten beaned pretty badly, but it looks nearly healed."

"Snow packs work wonders," Gerald said. "If we'd had the accident is the summer, I wouldn't have been able to take care of Merrill quite as well." The lady opened her back and unrolled a length of gauze, wrapping it around

Merrill's head. "Does he still need that if he's doing so well?"

"A precaution, that's all," she answered. "I want to protect his injury until we get him checked out at the hospital."

"Is a hospital really necessary? We just want to get back home to South Dakota."

"He might be hurt worse than it looks. Of course, it's up to you guys. I'm just a medical professional."

Merrill looked at Gerald. "It couldn't hurt. At least we'll be out of here. Hospitals have heat."

"Okay, you've sold me," Gerald grinned.

"You should get looked at too," the woman told Gerald. "You want to be sure you're okay."

Gerald moved across the floor to his luggage, pulled out a dry pair of socks and pulled them on. His black dress shoes followed. In no time, both men were standing and ready to leave.

The officers helped them down the path. What Merrill had dug continued past his work, having been scooped out by the police when they made their way to the shack.

They closed the cabin's door behind them. Gerald spent a second looking at the dilapidated but still serviceable structure, thankful it had been there to shelter them in their time of need.

He then walked along with the police, the paramedic, and Merrill, luggage in hand, through the woods toward the highway.

A tow truck had already moved the Crown Victoria out of the snowbank back onto the roadway's shoulder. Snow caked every bit of the car, making it look quite pathetic. "Sorry, old girl," Gerald whispered to it as he joined Merrill in the back of the ambulance.

He watched it disappear in the distance as they drove away. He loved that car. It was a classic, and had seen him through a lot of his life.

Just like Merrill.

Life had a funny way of showing a man what should be important to him.

All he had to do was listen.

Eleven

Merrill's checkup at the hospital took relatively little time. It seemed as if the ambulance ride from the cabin to the hospital lasted a lot longer than his visit with the emergency room techs. All the while, Gerald never left his side.

The nurses were impressed by how well Merrill's bump was taken care of with nothing more than snow. It was like a miracle that he responded to it so well.

Once Merrill was released, the two men wandered out of the hospital into the crisp late afternoon Idaho air. They stopped beneath the domed metallic canopy over the emergency entrance. "Well, what now?" Merrill asked.

"We get home, I guess," Gerald replied.

"How?"

Almost as soon as this question was uttered, around the bend in the driveway came Gerald's Crown Victoria, driven by one of the policemen who rescued them. Behind the car was a police cruiser.

They came to a stop in front of the pair. The car looked better than Gerald had seen it a long time. It had been cleaned up, washed, and any damage to the front end was repaired, virtually imperceptibly. The man got out of the car and walked around to them, handing Gerald the keys.

Gerald stammered. "What... how...?"

"Courtesy of the Boise P.D.," the officer said.

"Repairs must have cost a bundle."

"Perry McCann pitched in a significant amount of the repair charges when he heard the two of you are alright. You both must mean an awful lot to his company for him to put up so much money."

"We'll have to make sure to thank him," Merrill said.

"If relief could be felt through a phone line, we'd have felt it," the man said with a smile. "He'd been pretty worried when you guys didn't show up at the meeting."

"Which is long over by now," Gerald mused.

"Yes, it is," the officer said. He walked back to the car and opened the passenger door, withdrawing a manila envelope, thick with papers inside. He handed it to Gerald. "When they heard about your predicament, the men in charge made sure to put together a complete set of notes, proposals, and such for you to take back to South Dakota with you."

Gerald and Merrill exchanged a look.

"It's been an... interesting trip," Gerald said.

"I've never had one like it," Merrill commented.

"Nor are we likely to again."

The officer in the cruiser beeped his horn quickly to hurry the other policeman along. He acknowledged the prompt and gave the men a salute, turned, and climbed into the cruiser. In another moment, the police car was gone.

"Well, get in, Merr," Gerald said, holding the door open for his friend. "We have a long trip home ahead of us."

"Before you even ask, Gerry, no, I don't want to drive," Merrill said, buckling his seat belt.

Gerald assumed his place behind the steering wheel and started the car. "I don't blame you."

"I may never drive again."

"Not every car wants to kill you, buddy."

"Yours certainly tried."

"It had a little help from Mother Nature, and it still didn't succeed."

They pulled out of the parking area and headed for the street that would take them back to the highway out of Boise for the long drive back to Newford, South Dakota.

* * *

Fortunately, very little snow fell on them as they traversed the countryside between Idaho, Wyoming, into South Dakota. The roads remained mostly clear, and with a couple rest stops for restroom needs and gas and food along the way, they were relieved to see the city limits of Newford appear ahead of them.

They hadn't talk much during the drive. Merrill spent a lot of time sleeping against his door. Few cars passed them on the highway, reminding Gerald of those post-apocalyptic movies where the roadways were empty.

Gerald's mind was occupied most of the time with what had happened with Merrill. He glanced over at his softly slumbering best friend. He couldn't help but smile, despite his mind saying it shouldn't have happened, they should never have had sex. But he admitted in the deepest part of his heart and soul that he enjoyed it. He refused to deny it, especially to himself.

It happened, and he liked it.

In spite of what his mind was trying to convince him of, his heart told him that sharing his body with Merrill was alright.

He trusted his heart.

He trusted Merrill.

Hell, he *loved* Merrill. More than he ever did before, and in a totally different way.

He reached over and took the other man's hand and gave it squeeze. Merrill tiredly squeezed back, moaning in his sleep.

Pulling up into Merrill's driveway, Gerald turned off the car and looked at him. "You're home," he said gently, shaking his friend's shoulder to rouse him.

Merrill awoke, blinking in disbelief at the sight of his own house. "To think I almost thought I'd never set eyes on it again."

"Things looked bleak there for a while."

"You didn't give up."

"Neither did you."

"It's the most beautiful sight I've ever seen," Merrill said. He looked at Gerald with a wink, "Well, *one* of the most beautiful."

"Flatterer," Gerald said, faking a frown.

They exited the car and opened the trunk, taking Merrill's baggage out and lugging it to the front door. Merrill found his key and opened the door, stepping into the welcomed heat inside. He set his suitcase down on the tile entry floor beside the bags Gerald already put down.

"Some adventure," Gerald said, hands in his jacket's pockets.

"I'll say," Merrill replied with a whistle. "Remind me never to try to drive in snow again, okay?"

"You got it," Gerald grinned, clapping the other man on the shoulder. "I'll be having second thoughts about it for a long while myself."

They spent a few moments standing in the foyer, staring at each other. No words needed spoken. They knew how the other felt, how they felt about their new relationship.

Even if they were never naked together again, they had an experience that meant the world to them both. Looking back on it from a distance, it didn't seem as awkward or unnatural as either had thought it did at the time. After all, they had a lifetime of knowing each other and being friends to prepare for it, even if they had no idea it was going to happen.

"Well, I'd better get home and let you get some rest," Gerald said finally.

"I slept most of the way back, but I feel like I didn't get any sleep at all."

"You've got a nice soft bed and warm blankets to sleep in now," Gerald said. "No more ratty, dirty rug and skimpy beach blanket."

"At least you have a warm body to go home too," Merrill pointed out. "Melanie has to have been worried sick about you."

"I imagine so."

He held his arms out, inviting Merrill into them for a hug. Merrill stepped forward, wrapping his own arms around Gerald's torso, holding him close. They stood there for several minutes, motionless, just enjoying the feel of the other man. Being together was something they'd always loved before. Now, it felt even more personal, more genuine, more loving.

Gerald kissed the side of Merrill's head. Merrill laid a kiss on Gerald's neck.

Hesitantly, they broke the embrace. Without a word, Gerald turned, opened the door, and left, closing it after him. Merrill watched him through the window, getting into the Crown Victoria, starting the engine, and backing out of the driveway. Seconds later, he was gone.

Merrill picked up his luggage and toted it into his bedroom and sank down on the bed on his back. His fingers intertwined behind his head, he stared at the ceiling. Memories of their time inside the cabin kept flashing across his mind, mostly the way Gerald took care of his wound and was so attentive and nursing.

When the thoughts of Gerald undressing him in front of the fire came, he felt like the luckiest man in the world. A lifelong dream he'd always longed to come true actually did. He was able to make love to Gerald Millard, his favorite person on the face of the planet.

It had been all he hoped for, maybe even more. It was heartbreakingly real. It really happened. He could almost still smell Gerald's scent lingering around him as he lay on his bed.

Being together so intimately may never happen a second time, but Merrill had the memory of the one time that it did to hold onto.

He loved Gerald even more.

He was sure Gerald felt the same.

He hoped.

Twelve

Melanie was at the front door when Gerald pulled up in their driveway. She knew the eccentric rattles and other sounds that made the Crown Victoria uniquely Gerald's. She ran to the door and flung it open just in time to see him pull to a stop.

She contained herself just long enough for him to reach the top of the front steps before throwing her arms around him, kissing him over and over. "Oh, honey, oh baby," she said over and over as she held him tight.

"I'm home," he finally said. He looked deep in his wife's emerald green eyes that offset her curly red hair so well. "I'm home."

"Are you alright, honey? Is Merrill?" she asked, sliding his jacket off him and escorting him into the living room and sitting him down on his favorite chair.

"I'm fine. So is Merrill, though he did get quite a knock on the head when the car went off the road," he explained.

"You're home now, home and well." She cuddled up against her husband and closed her eyes, relieved to have him back. "When Mr. McCann said you never showed up to the Boise meeting, I feared the worst."

"Believe me, so did we."

"I heard that was the worst snowfall in forty years," she said. "I tried not to imagine... not to think about... oh, Gerald, I'm so glad you're finally home."

He put an arm around her shoulders and rubbed her arm. "We found an old abandoned cabin and took shelter there."

"Still, it had to be horrible."

He nodded.

"Were you at least able to make a fire and stay warm?" she asked.

"Most of the wood was too wet to burn, but we managed."

"I'm glad."

They sat in silence a few minutes. She ran her hand over his chest. She listened intently to the sound of his heartbeat.

Gerald tossed around his brain the idea of telling his wife what happened between him and Merrill, unable to convince himself whether telling her about his sexuality was a good thing or a bad thing.

He liked sex with Merrill.

He loved sex with Melanie.

He was happy with him as well as with her, but they two were distinctly different.

His sexuality prior to Melanie had never come up. It was a subject that he didn't feel was relevant once he was with her. The men, women, and couples he'd spent time with before Melanie were little more than memories.

That's how they should remain.

But revisiting his bisexuality in Merrill Bostwick's arms was very relevant to him now. He'd sworn when they got married never to keep secrets from his wife. Was this a possible exception to that vow?

A fleeting image of Merrill's unclothed body in the firelight shot across Gerald's vision. He had a monumental decision to make.

Should Gerald tell Melanie about having sex with Merrill?

* *If you think he should, read on to* chapter **13**.

* *If you think he shouldn't, go to the "Alternate Ending" chapter.*

Thirteen

Gerald decided to tell Melanie what happened between him and Merrill. He didn't like the thought of it eating at him in the coming years and felt he owed it to her. She was a wonderful woman and a loving wife. She'd stood beside him in trying times before. Nothing they had withstood together in the past came close to what he was facing right now. There was no telling if this storm could be weathered or not. But he wanted to try.

"Mel, can we talk?" he asked quietly.

"Mm-hmm," she purred, snuggling closer to his chest. He moved his hand from her shoulder to stroke her hair.

"I mean *really* talk."

She sat up and gazed at him. "That certainly sounds ominous."

He looked away and clasped his hands together between his knees. He felt his face prickle with redness as he battled inwardly over what he was about to do.

"I love you," he said.

Melanie sat back against the back of the couch, her mouth agape. "That's never a good way to start a conversation, especially after a weekend away."

He said nothing.

"Did something happen? I know there was an accident, yes, but did something else happen?" she said measuredly.

He slowly nodded. He purposefully avoided looking at her, signaling Melanie that whatever was coming was going to be bad.

"You can tell me anything, Gerry, no matter how... how bad it is," she prodded, stumbling in uncertainty. "There's nothing that bad..."

"I had sex with Merrill."

Her jaw dropped open further. Her eyes narrowed as she regarded him. Melanie reached forward, took her husband by the chin, and turned his head to face her. "I know I can't have heard you right."

He looked into her eyes, his own ready to spout a torrent of tears.

"You... and Merrill Bostwick..." she said haltingly, "you two had sex. This past weekend."

Gerald nodded again, snuffling his nose. He was fighting so hard not to cry.

"How is such a thing even possible?" she demanded, getting to her feet and standing over him.

He shrugged, looking down at his shoes. "It just, kind of, happened."

"You and Merrill...?"

He finally looked up at her. "Yes, me and Merrill."

"I don't even know where to start with the questions," she exclaimed.

"I'm not sure I even have any answers."

"First off, how could you have sex with a man? You're straight and married to me. That's two strikes already!"

He put his hands up in surrender. "There are maybe one or two things you never knew about me, Melanie, things I've kept in my past. I don't know why."

"Well, start with the most important one then," she said. "Are you gay?"

"No, no, no, no, no I'm not," he said hurriedly.

"Having sex with a man means you're gay, Gerald," she said firmly.

"I... I'm bisexual, honey. I always have been," he confessed, putting his hands in front of his face.

"'Bisexual'?"

"Yes, bisexual," he answered. "I've been with both men and women in sexual situations. I'm sorry I've never mentioned it before. I never thought my life before you mattered. It's not who I am anymore."

"Apparently that isn't true if you've recently been sexual with Merrill Bostwick." She was holding herself together remarkably well, what with the stream of new information she was being given.

"It was the first time in over twenty years, Mel," he protested. "The first time since I met you. Since then, I have been nothing but faithful to you."

"And with your own best friend," she moaned.

Gerald took her hand and drew her back onto the couch beside him. "I know it's a lot to take in, too much for you to understand all at once. I get that. I really do."

"I'm not sure you do."

She slid her hand out of his and crossed her arms, looking into the middle of the room, unable to look at him. Her face was expressionless as if she were trying to turn herself to stone.

Without preamble, Gerald Millard launched into his explanation of what had gone on after he left the house to head to Idaho. He told her how he had driven most of the way, then surrendered the driver's seat to Merrill, who was uncomfortable driving in snow. He told her how the car lost control and left the road, plowing into a snow bank several yards off the highway, out of sight of passing vehicles.

Gerald explained how he found the cabin and retrieved Merrill, carried him through the woods to shelter. How he tended Merrill's wound, gathered firewood, and did his best to keep them alive. When he got to the part where the men came out as bisexual to each other, he faltered for a moment before continuing the story.

He told her how they were huddling together to share body heat, as they'd learned in the Boy Scouts as youngsters.

She looked away when he mentioned them disrobing. Not going into lurid details, he went on with his story to the point of them trying to call for help by tramping HELP in the snow.

"None of this explains why sex came into the picture," she interrupted.

"It shouldn't have," he admitted. "It was a heat of the moment thing. We weren't sure we were ever going to make it out of that cabin alive. That's no good excuse for anything, but it happened."

Melanie sighed. Her emotions were raging a war inside her. Gerald could see that plainly.

"So... why tell me? Why not keep it dirty little secret like you did about your bisexuality?" She finally looked at him, pleading for comprehending in her eyes. "You didn't have to tell me any of this. You could have gone on happily without saying a word."

"You know why I had to tell you," he retorted. "I have more integrity than that. It's not who I am. I'm in love with my wife, with *you*, Melanie."

"You were you in that cabin with Merrill too," she shot back.

"That was a different person," he stated.

"It's still you, Gerald."

"Can we get past this, please?" he begged.

Melanie looked at him, at his worried face, at his quivering mustache and clenched hands. He had no real right to ask her to forgive, let alone forget.

"Please," he whispered, bowing his head.

She felt her will break. She had never seen this side of her husband. In all the years she'd known him, Melanie never knew this fragile part of Gerald existed. She wasn't certain she liked it. He was always a strong, capable man. Very little could ever bother him.

She reached out and stroked his hair tenderly. He gave a soft sob at her touch.

He raised his face to look at her, a tear running down his cheek. Melanie had to admit to herself, she was never more in love with Gerald than she was at that moment. He was being his true self, the man she always knew he was deep inside but was unwilling to show her.

She leaned in and gave him a gentle kiss. Now he openly wept, relief gushing out of him. He threw his arms around his wife and pulled her close.

At supper later that evening, they sat at the dinner table, eating microwaved TV dinners. She didn't want to cook. He didn't want to eat out. They compromised and raided the freezer. As they finished eating, she looked across the table at him and gave a half smile.

"What?" Gerald asked.

"In all my life, I never would have suspected. Never once."

"I promise there will never be any more secrets," he swore. "I will be an open book from now on."

She nodded, setting her fork down on the aluminum tray in from of her. "That's good, and I'm going to hold you to that."

He nodded enthusiastically.

"There's still one thing I don't quite understand," she said, cupping his hands in her own.

"Only one thing?" he asked, jaw open. "I must have made a better explanation than I thought."

"Of all the people – all the men – you could have been bisexual with, now or ever, why Merrill Bostwick?"

"We've been best friends all our lives."

"And you've never had sex with him before?"

"No, I never knew he was bi, or even liked men, before this weekend. Why?"

"Did he know about you?"

"No, neither of us knew anything about the other."

"Despite being best friends all your lives."

"Yes."

"So the subject of bisexuality *never* came up?"

"If it did, I can't remember," he said.

"It could be worse, I suppose," she declared.

"How's that?"

"It could have been a total stranger," she said, "or one of those weird sex party orgies I've heard about. You never know who's been where with who."

"I trust Merrill implicitly, my love," Gerald said categorically. "And just to clear the air before you ask, I have never been in an orgy. Twosomes and threesomes, yes, but never an orgy."

She smiled. "I feel a little better now."

"So do I," he said. He caressed the backs of her hands with his thumbs the way she liked him too. "I'm so *so* sorry it happened, but thank you for not throwing me out over this."

"You have some making-up to do, mister," Melanie told him. She rose from her chair and walked around the table, seating herself on his lap. She kissed his forehead lovingly. "I do love you. You know that."

"I do."

"It's going to be pretty difficult to put this in the past, but I'm willing to try."

"So am I."

They kissed. It was a completely unlike kind of kiss than he'd shared with Merrill, but this was his wife, and he was where he belonged.

THE END

Alternate Ending

Gerald decided not to tell Melanie what happened between him and Merrill. He was just happy to be home, and she felt so good lying against him that he told himself that the entire weekend must have been nothing but a bad dream.

It didn't hhappen.

He never drove to Idaho, never slid off the road in a blizzard, certainly never had sex with Merrill Bostwick. It couldn't have happened. Everything he wanted in life was sitting there on the couch with him.

Melanie.

Yet, it did happen. No matter how strongly Gerald tried to deny it to himself, he *had* gone on the business trip to Idaho, there *was* an accident in the blizzard, and yes, he and Merrill *did* make love in front of a fireplace in a deserted old cabin.

No amount of disavowal could change the reality of what he'd done.

It was best not to let Melanie worry over something that happened once and would never happen again.

But could he be sure he would never seek pleasure from Merrill again? They *were* best friends, after all, and they *did* work together at the same firm. They would be seeing each other every day. How long could they allow the awkward glances back and forth to continue before one of them broke?

Gerald kissed Melanie on top of her head and rubbed her arm lovingly. "I love you so much," he whispered.

"Mmm, I love you too," she cooed.

* * *

It wasn't long before Gerald got a promotion in the company, and soon after that, Perry McCann retired, leaving McCann Electronics in Gerald capable hands. He proved to be a fair and wise voice for the firm. He elevated Merrill to become his personal assistant, a fact which incensed a couple of other employees who thought they deserved the job more.

Unfortunately, this was the time when rumors began to circulate, touting the men's close friendship as being something far more intimate. Whispers and giggles went around the building like wildfire. In no time, speculations that Gerald and Merrill were lovers spread through the company, and soon, people started purposefully avoiding both of them. If they didn't need to speak to them, they stayed far afield of the two.

One evening when Gerald got home from work, he found Melanie standing on the front porch waiting for him. She didn't look pleased. He got out of his car and walked up the steps to greet her.

She turned her face away when he tried to kiss her hello.

"What's wrong, buttercup?" he asked, confused.

"Is it true?" she demanded in return.

"Is *what* true? I have no idea what you're talking about."

"We can stand out here all night if you want," she said, sternly. "I have all night."

"Why don't give me a clue what you're asking me so I know how to answer?"

"One of your employees called me today with some, let's call it *interesting*, news."

He looked at her dumbfounded. What had she heard that would bother her this much? Nothing had happened recently that *he* knew of. Melanie was sweet as sugar that morning when he left. Something happened during the day.

"What exactly happened on your business trip to Boise, Idaho?" she asked pointedly.

"You know all that," he replied. "We skidded off the road in a snowstorm and had to shelter in a cabin until we were rescued. I told you all this when I got home."

"There appear to be some details you left out of your story," Melanie said harshly.

Oh no...

"Now, honey, you know..."

"So I want to know, here and now, if the rumors I've been hearing all afternoon are true," she insisted. "Are they or are they not true?"

Gerald felt trapped. Even in the cool of the evening, he was perspiring. He was totally unprepared for a confrontation, but it seemed like his wife was more than up for it.

Somehow she knew.

"What have you heard?" he asked tentatively.

Melanie set her jaw and glared at him. "What have I heard? Where should I begin?"

He shrugged, knowing that no matter what he said, she would misconstrue and turn it against him. "Wherever you want to," he replied.

She planted her body squarely between Gerald and the door into the house. Her stance was combative in an uncompromising way. Her balled-up fists were on her hips. "Let's start with an easy one, shall we? What exactly happened in that cabin between you and Merrill Bostwick?"

"I don't know what you mean, honey..."

"Don't ever try lying to me, Gerald Quincy Millard," she raged. "I know a lot more than you seem to think I do. So try being honest with me, okay? Is that too much for a wife to ask of her husband?"

Gerald's eyes shot around the porch, looking for something to focus on and gather courage from.

He found nothing.

"Did you have sex with him?" she asked point blank, observing his reaction for validation. The unintentional widening of his eyes in surprise gave him away.

"You did, didn't you? You and Merrill had sex together. Don't deny it, I can read it all over your face."

He lowered his head and clasped his hands behind his back. He muttered affirmation.

"I didn't quite hear you."

"I said, yes, we did. Alright? Merrill and I started out huddling together to keep warm in an ice-cold shack in the middle of nowhere. It got a little out of hand. It wasn't like we planned it, okay? It just happened."

"And you decided not to tell me about it?"

"Judging from your reaction right now, yeah, I didn't see a need to mention it, because I knew you'd be exactly like this," Gerald countered. "You know you have my heart, Melanie."

"But this weekend, someone else had your body," she retorted. "Your best friend, no less. Well, I hope he was worth it. I really hope that."

"It didn't mean anything," Gerald said frantically.

She turned her back on him, crossing her arms against the cool of nightfall. "I'm sure it didn't."

"It didn't!" he insisted.

She swung around again to fix a fierce gaze on him. "Then why did you feel a need not to tell me?"

"You want me to tell you I was unfaithful during a business trip?" he asked, astounded. "That's how so many divorces get started."

"You were unfaithful to me with a *man*, Gerald! How am I supposed to feel about that? Being replaced in your love life by another man?"

"You're not even trying to understand..."

"I understand all that I need to very well," Melanie cried into the night air. "I understand that you had sex with another man and decided to lie to me about it."

"I never lied about it."

"It was a lie of exclusion," she said icily. "You kept it from me deliberately and maliciously."

"There was no malice..."

"Just get back in your car, Gerald," she said stiffly. "Get in your precious Crown Victoria and take your sorry self over to Merrill. Maybe he'll have you. I sure won't. You've made mistakes in the past, and I've been very forgiving.

"This time, the hurt is too much. I can't bear it." She was weeping now. Gerald gallantly fought back his own tears, longing to hold his wife and soothe their mutual pain away.

But he couldn't move.

"You can come by for your things," Melanie said, opening the door and stepping inside. "I can't even look at you anymore."

"Melanie honey, I love you," he cried at the closed door. "Only you..."

Defeated, he got back into his car, backed out of his driveway, and headed down the street. He was tempted to drive around the neighborhood for hours, praying that Melanie would change her mind and call his cell phone and ask him to come home.

Instead, he found himself parked at Merrill's house, looking at the lit lamp in the living room from the chilly solitude of the driveway. Compared to where he'd just been, it seemed to beckon him, welcomingly.

He knocked on Merrill's door.

"Gerry," Merrill said, shocked at his friend's sudden, unexpected appearance on his doorstep. "What are you doing here?"

Gerald let a tear escape his eye. "Can I come in, Merr? I need to talk to you."

THE (other) END

Printed in Great Britain
by Amazon

44791467R00081